Please return / renew by date shown.
You can renew it at:

Starry Nights, STAGE FRIGHT and my Surprise Valentine

STRIPES PUBLISHING
An imprint of Magi Publications
1 The Coda Centre, 189 Munster Road, London SW6 6AW

A paperback original

ISBN:

First published in Great Britain

978-1-84715-108-7

in 2009 Text copyright © Liz Elwes, 2009 The right of Liz Elwes to
be identified as the author of this work has been asserted by her in
accordance with the Copyright, Designs and Patents Act, 1988. All
rights reserved. A CIP catalogue record for this book is available
from the British Library. This book is sold subject to the condition
Printed and bound in Belgium.
10 9 8 7 6 5 4 3 2 1

To Giles, William, Alice, Thomas and Jamie, and all my good friends for all
their patience and understanding during the writing of this book.
To Janice Swanson and Stephanie Thwaites at Curtis Brown for all
their support, and to Jane Harris and everyone at Stripes.

Crush
confidential

Starry Nights,
STAGE
FRIGHT
and my
Surprise
Valentine

Liz Elwes

Stripes

"She's going to make an announcement." Rosie nodded. "Look at her, rocking on her black lace-ups – it's obvious. She's got something important to say." She gave me a nudge. "What do you think it is?"

"Someone's been caught snogging behind the science labs *again*?" I said innocently, turning round to look at Lola.

"Hey!" she protested. "It wasn't me, Isabel! I'd dropped an earring and Joe was just helping me look for it."

"Behind your tonsils?" Rosie enquired. Lola and I giggled.

I leaned back in my chair and tried to get comfortable. I knew we wouldn't be going anywhere for hours. The first assembly of term always goes on for ever.

I stretched out my legs and began to flex my feet ... good toes, naughty toes, good toes, naughty toes.

It was quite hard in my brand-new shoes. They were black and had the highest heel that Mum would allow me and I loved them – but as my feet were usually tucked inside dance shoes of one description or another, any proper shoes felt like boulders tied to the bottom of my legs.

"What are you doing?" asked Rosie, staring down at my feet. "Ah, are you making up a little dance?" she cooed.

"Ha ha, very funny. I'm doing nothing, actually, that's what I'm doing. I'm minding my own business. Not like some people," I whispered meaningfully. "Your head's been swivelling like … like an owl."

Rosie stopped swivelling and fixed me with mock disbelief. "Isabel, I'm going to be *an actress* – I need to observe people." She flicked back her red hair. "It's part of the job. Ask me what I've already learned this morning while you've been doing your imaginary dance routine. Go on … ask me!"

I waited as the Year Sevens wandered past us in a shambolic line, their mindless chatter immediately silenced at the sight of the majestic Mrs Hampton-Smith up on stage. Rosie was right, you could tell that she had something important to say. The Year Nines were streaming in now, crashing and bumping as they sat down in the row in front of us.

I faked a yawn. "All right. Go on then, Miss Drama Queen," I replied, "what *have* you found out?"

Rosie began ticking off her fingers. "Bryony Page has had her hair cut really short. *Really* suits her. Mariah has put red extensions in her hair." She shook her head. "*Big* mistake. Toby is still loving Julie from afar – look, he's just given her one of his longing looks. When is he ever going to pluck up the courage and ask her out...?" She pulled out her shirt and squinted down. "And my frontage growth over the holidays has been very disappointing."

"Ekk, ekk, ekk..." From the seat next to her came a noise similar to a small cat retching up a fur ball.

We both turned to look.

Missako was making contorted faces and uttering little bird-like cries.

She saw us staring and stopped.

"Oops! Sorry ... just warming up. First singing lesson straight after drama."

I do not seem to have normal friends like other people.

But not many people *are* normal at our school. I leaned forward and looked down our row. It was full of people who wanted to be actors and dancers and singers. Linden Lodge is a school for the performing arts, which is why it is full of divas, artistic types and mammoth personalities. Here, everything is always a drama!

And talking of drama, why did it have to be the first lesson after this? There aren't that many shy girls at Linden Lodge, but unfortunately I'm one of them and a drama lesson is *not* my idea of a good time. My brother's nickname for me is "Mouse", because I'm pretty timid and I get anxious about the smallest of things. And I know I'm not the best at speaking up; I tend to wait to hear what others say first, just in case I make a fool out of myself. That's why I love being friends with Rosie – she's always happy to lead the way.

Suddenly, all thoughts of ballet shoes, drama and mad friends flew out of the window. My heart started to pound like a drum, my face flushed the colour of tomato ketchup and I swiftly tucked all my toes, good and naughty, under my chair. Because none other than Charlie Rothwell had sat down in the seat right in front of me. And I mean *right* in front – my knees were practically touching his chair. If I'd wanted to I could have reached out and stroked his hair. Which I sort of did want to as it was long and dark blond and gorgeous. But of course I didn't. Charlie Rothwell is in the year above and is one of the coolest boys in the school. He majors in drama, but sings brilliantly and always gets great roles in our school productions, which, as we're a performing arts school, means quite a lot of roles.

And I was mad about him.

I had been mad about him for approximately 469 days. Which means since my second day at Linden Lodge. All the new girls were whispering about him. He wasn't just seriously good-looking, he was seriously funny and nice to everyone as well. Which made him definitely one of the most popular boys in his year. At first I'd just sighed whenever he walked past, but I was more mature now, which meant I simply lost the power of speech and went scarlet any time he came near me. There was a world of difference.

Sadly I was not alone in my passion. I suspected his stunning girlfriend Laura quite liked him, too, followed by, oooh, pretty much all the girls in the school.

That's why I'd kept my feelings a secret, even from Rosie and Missako. I didn't want them to tease me about it. It was my private fantasy that I hugged to myself. The one in which one day the school heart-throb would notice me and sweep me off my feet. And be my first kiss.

Everyone else in our year except Missako and me seemed to be kissing people all over the place. I was getting worried I might be the last in the school – and lusting after hopelessly inaccessible Charlie wasn't going to help. Charlie's girlfriend, the beautiful Laura Baines, must be the happiest girl in the whole world going out with him. I dragged my eyes away from the back of Charlie's head and scanned his row to find her.

Whoah! I surely would have looked a lot happier than *that* anyway! She looked positively annoyed – and I thought she kept that look just for me. Although she's the year above, the best dancers in our year share a couple of classes with her year and she hates it. And she especially doesn't like *me* as I'm a scholarship girl. My parents aren't exactly poor, but they've got four children and could never afford to send me here if I hadn't won one of the assisted places in our year.

Rosie has one of the others. I know Laura looks down her pretty turned-up nose at us. I can hear her very loud whispers about "scholarship kids" from right across the rehearsal rooms.

I jumped. Suddenly everyone was clapping and cheering. I stared around, confused.

Rosie and Missako beamed at me. "Isn't it great?" Missako whooped.

"What? What's great?" I asked, bewildered.

"The Valentine's Prom, of course. Weren't you listening? Isabel! You missed the big announcement!"

"It's going to be based on an American High School Prom to tie in with this term's production of *Grease*." Rosie sighed, pressing her hand on her heart. "And it's going to be on Valentine's Day – how romantic is that? Oh, what *will* I wear? And more importantly, who will ask me to go with them?"

I saw more than one of the boys around us already glancing in her direction and guessed Rosie would have nothing to worry about on that score. With her red hair, stunning green eyes and fabulous long legs she's never had trouble attracting attention. She's had three boyfriends already and gets asked out on dates all the time. She's always pushing me to be more confident. She reckons if I believed in myself a little bit more the boys would flock around me as well. It's great that she thinks that, but the more she pushes the more nervous I become. Anyway, I was only interested in one boy, and he was sitting inches away from me.

Mrs Hampton-Smith settled everyone down and eventually, after about a year, assembly was over and the hall began to empty, row by row. Charlie stood up and as he did so he turned round to face us. His brown eyes ran over Rosie, Missako and me and he broke into a broad smile. "Sounds good, doesn't it?"

I stared back in stunned silence. Charlie Rothwell was talking to *me*. "The Prom I mean," he went on. "Sounds good."

"Sounds absolutely brilliant!" Rosie cried merrily. "Will you be auditioning…" But Charlie had already turned back, nudged by the next boy in his row, and shuffled off.

We had left the hall and had nearly made it to the drama studio when class gossips Sadia and Chelsea came running up behind us. "Did we see Charlie

Rothwell talking to you? Because guess what? Guess what? Guess what?!"

Rosie held open the studio door and we ducked in under her arm. "What?!" she yelled.

"He's finished with Laura! They've split up." Sadia and Chelsea positively burst with excitement at delivering such important news.

"Split up," I gasped, my heart pounding. "How…?"

"Really?" Missako asked. "How do you know?"

"It's all over the school; he ended it in the holidays. It's totally over. You must have seen her sat there with her I've-just-eaten-a-lemon face in assembly?" Sadia gasped. "Oh my goodness, you know what this means?" She steadied herself on Chelsea's arm and put the back of her hand to her forehead in a mock swoon.

"What?" asked Rosie.

"This means that Charlie Rothwell does *not* have a date for the Valentine's Prom. Oh. My. God. I mean, who, who, *who* is he going to take now?"

"Isabel! You have just discovered that Danny, your wonderful summer romance, is a pupil at your new school... Imagine! You suddenly look up and see the boy who you thought you would never see again standing right in front of you." Mr Anderson stroked his trendy little beard, and his black brows furrowed. "You *are* aware of the story of *Grease* I take it?"

I nodded dumbly. My mouth felt dry. This was *exactly* why I hated drama – I was no good at it, and Mr Anderson never let *anyone* get away with not performing. We were all dragged out to the centre of the huge studio floor in turn.

"So why have you just greeted Danny, thank you, Gus, lovely job, with as much excitement as if you saw him every day of your life and had just bumped into him at the supermarket?"

I remained silent. How could I be expected to act

anything when not only did it frighten the life out of me, but all I could think about was Charlie? I had made a big decision as soon as I'd heard the news. At break time, I was going to tell Rosie and Missako my secret. I was going to speak out. No more shy Isabel, the one who got the worst stage fright in the year. This was the beginning of a new confident me, the one Rosie said she knew was in me all along. I couldn't wait for the class to end. Rosie and Missako were leaning against the wall with the rest of the group, having watched my feeble effort to act a scene from *Grease* with Gus. Rosie was still loyally making encouraging thumbs-up signs at me and mouthing "Brilliant!" in spite of all the evidence to the contrary.

"Well?" Mr Anderson tapped his foot.

"I could *dance* being pleased to see him," I offered, looking at the floor. "I think that might help me put some more emotion into it." At least then I wouldn't have to speak.

Mr Anderson closed his eyes as if in pain. He opened them again, adjusted the little scarf around his neck, and placed a hand on my shoulder. "The thing is, Isabel, the thing is ... I'm sure we would all LOVE to see you

dance – I'm sure it would be quite the most wonderful dance we have ever seen – but the problem is that when I last saw a stage production of *Grease*, which *I believe* is what we are trying to achieve this term, it did require some…" and at this point his hand made a flourishing gesture "… *words*."

I nodded. I couldn't disagree with that. But Mr Anderson was on a roll now.

"We could of course do it as a mime, a ballet with no speaking and no songs. But I think our audience here at Linden Lodge might be the tiniest bit disappointed not to have a song or two. It would be a bit like going to see *Swan Lake* and a member of the corps de ballet popping their head around the curtain and saying, 'Hey! Just to let you know we've had a chat amongst ourselves and we've decided to do a non-dancing version tonight and sing a few songs about birds instead.' Mmm? What do you say, Isabel?"

There was the sound of stifled giggles from the rest of the class.

"It was only a suggestion."

"Next couple, please."

Rosie and Finn ran into the centre of the room.

"And another thing," Mr Anderson called after me. "You will be working with the partner I've given you this morning until half-term. Then I will be able to see you pro-*gress* and *de*-vel-op your techniques."

Terrific. I pulled a face and mumbled an apology to Gus, who looked delighted. He had had a bit of a crush on me for a while – well, not just me, any girl really – and wasn't that good at taking the hint. Now I would be acting love scenes with him, listening to him doing that enthusiastic breathing he does way too close. Missako gave me a sympathetic glance and I flattened myself against the wall next to her to watch Rosie. Missako had acted earlier with Fred. They had been good so she was relaxed now, her ordeal was over.

Of course Rosie was brilliant. In fact today she was almost on fire, fizzing with even more excitement and energy than usual. You truly believed that she adored stocky, hatchet-faced Finn and meeting him was the most thrilling experience of her life, when in fact I know she thinks Finn's big-headed and arrogant, which he is. He's a good actor but not a generous one. Rosie, on the other hand, looked like she was riveted by every line he spoke.

Missako leaned towards me and whispered, "You *would* have been able to dance it beautifully."

I gave her a rueful smile and shrugged. "Maybe, but let's face it," I sighed, "I may not mind dancing but when it comes to nearly everything else, you and Rosie are officially friends with a mouse. Don't deny it. I know that's what everyone thinks of me."

"Rubbish! I *had* a mouse, remember? A white one. Remember Angelina? I tried hanging out with her for a while and believe me she wasn't anything like as funny and interesting as you."

"I bet she could act, though."

"Ah, well, yes. Brilliantly. In fact she won a mouse Oscar."

"Don't tell me, for the lead in *Squeaking Beauty*."

We dissolved into giggles. And for the millionth time I felt lucky that Missako and Rosie were my best friends.

"It's not fair that most of the lead parts will probably go to the year above, is it?" Missako sighed. "Rosie would be wonderful as Sandy. And Fred would be a great Danny." Fred is the best actor in our class; with his dark hair and blue eyes, he'd certainly look the part. He's also a genuinely nice guy. The thought fleetingly popped into my head that Missako might be keen on him, but I had other things to think about.

"Everyone knows Charlie will be Danny," I said decisively. "And just because Laura got the lead role last term doesn't mean to say she's going to get it again. Autumn is in her West End show so she can't be in it." Autumn Monroe was easily the most glamorous girl in the year above, but now she was performing in London most of the time she was no longer in school that often. "So someone from our year could easily get it."

"Hmmm…" said Missako. "And what about Zack?" "He's in that year and he's got to be the best actor."

"Zack!" I snorted. Zack was in Charlie's year and they went round in the same crowd. His dad was the lead guitarist in a huge rock band. All the girls thought he was the coolest thing, but I didn't. I thought he was way too full of himself. "No," I said firmly, "it's got to be Charlie and, like I said, someone in our year *could* get Sandy."

I certainly hoped they would. I didn't like the idea of Laura and Charlie being thrown back together again for all those rehearsals. I looked round the drama studio. "Who else do you think stands a chance?" I asked, but what I really meant was, "Who else might be lucky enough to spend huge amounts of time acting love scenes with Charlie?"

Missako sighed. "Well, Lola has a great voice..." We looked over at a lithe, bright-eyed girl with black eye make-up and tumbling jet-black hair. I relaxed – Lola was way too scary. "...But I think she's more Rizzo than Sandy." I had to agree. "Then there's Sadia and Chelsea – loud enough and good actors, but again, not right for Sandy. And of course there's always Blue..." A large, athletic girl was limbering up on the sidelines of the drama studio, hopping from one foot to the other, desperate for her turn. Blue's father had made his money in supermarkets and had decided his daughter was born for the stage. He had pushed hard for her to come to Linden Lodge – in fact he had donated the funds for the very drama studio we were working in. He lovingly turned up to all the performances and never seemed to notice that his daughter had absolutely no talent at all; but then again, neither did she.

"They're bound to give her something," Joanna said spikily, eavesdropping as usual. "To keep Daddy sweet."

I frowned at this catty remark. Joanna was undoubtedly one of the most attractive girls in our year, but I'm sure the rest of us would have looked good if we'd had access to hair, clothes and make-up stylists. That's what life is like when your mother is the famous actress, Paige Madison. Joanna's dad disappeared years ago to Australia and her mum is often in Hollywood, so Joanna is looked after by a large staff whose only task is to do exactly as she says.

I didn't really care who got what part, except for Sandy and Danny, and seeing Rosie in action now, she looked born to play Sandy. Missako would definitely get a part, too. With her pretty face and shiny straight black hair, she sings like a dream and unlike me is loads more confident on stage than off it. I simply wanted to dance the hand-jive in a prom frock with a huge frothy skirt. We were going to be learning the moves in our modern dance class tomorrow.

Rosie and Finn finished and the class gave a spontaneous round of applause.

I waited for her to join us before whispering, "After this class, meeting, back of the music rooms, on the bench. I've something really important to tell you."

Rosie clapped her hands together and beamed. "Wow. More surprise announcements. I can't wait!"

"Well, what do you expect if you try to run on points in those shoes?" Rosie sighed as she held out a hand to haul me up.

"I just wanted to see if I could."

"Well, I think you've answered your own question," said Missako, picking up my bag from the corridor floor and handing it back to me.

I was furious with myself. "Why did I have to fall flat on my face in front of Laura Baines of all people? How can fate be so cruel?"

Rosie began to mimic Laura's smug tone. "Oh dear, Isabel, you'll have to do better than that if you're going to stand any chance of getting into *Madame's* group."

I groaned and dabbed a tissue on the small cut on my elbow.

"I don't know if it's really wise to let the younger *scholarship* girls try for it at all," Rosie continued, getting the way Laura flicks her hair down to perfection. "*Everyone*'s having extra tuition outside school for Madame's audition; it's simply *not* fair on those girls whose parents can't afford it."

"Yes, thank you for that, Rosie. I *do* remember what she said. I wish she wouldn't go on about my parents as if they lived in a hovel or something. Urgh…" I shook my head. "I'm going to see her in five minutes as well. She's in my next class."

"Well, that's your fault for being brilliant at ballet and being in her set and having a chance to audition for Madame's class. You're a star!" Rosie is nothing if not supportive. "If you were rubbish at ballet, like me, you wouldn't have these problems. I love, love, love modern but Miss Wright said my point work…" Rosie lifted a foot to demonstrate "…actually caused her physical…er… what was it?"

"Anguish," Missako offered. "It was 'physical anguish'. Now are we going to get to hear Isabel's news or not? Because if we're late for our next classes we will *all* suffer physical anguish from the earbashing we'll get."

Rosie jumped up and down. "Yes! Yes! Yes!" She pointed dramatically ahead. "To the bench!"

We pushed open the door into the crisp January air and walked out along the tree-lined path. The sounds of a violin and a jazz saxophone wafted out of rehearsal room windows as we arrived at our destination. The bench wasn't strictly ours, but we felt it was as good as. It was always quiet there.

"Right," said Rosie, flopping down. She stuck her long legs out in front of her and huddled her shoulder against mine. "Hurry up, it's freezing. What have you got to tell us?"

"We-ell…" I began, settling in between her and Missako. But then the words dried in my mouth, because walking along the path, with two other boys, was Charlie Rothwell. He slowed right down as he passed us and smiled.

"Hiya."

"Hiya," we chorused. He had smiled at me. Again! I watched him as he went past and disappeared into the school.

"We-ell…" I began again.

Rosie fell back, pretending to faint. "Isn't he totally, utterly gorgeous?"

I smiled. Rosie would say that about any good-looking

boy, but she hadn't finished yet. "I mean I'm sorry to interrupt, Isabel, but did you see that? That's the second time he's smiled at me today. It's got to mean something. Do you think he's been following us? In fact I've got something that I have to say to you two as well."

"What?" Missako's eyes were as round as saucers.

Rosie jumped up on the bench and stretched her arms heavenwards. "I'm totally crazy about Charlie Rothwell, and all I want in the whole wide world is for him to ask me to the Valentine's Prom…"

"But you never said…" I was struggling to get the words out.

Rosie beamed down at me. "I know! But when he was going out with Laura *nobody* thought they stood a chance, so I didn't *allow* myself to think about it. But now he's free and he's smiled at me twice in one morning. I think he really likes me. Oh my God, do you think I really could get him to invite me to the Prom? Promise me you'll do everything you can to help me? And imagine if I get the part of Sandy as well? It's like a match made in heaven. The best Valentine's Day ever. Oh, but hey!" She scrambled down next to me again.

"Listen to me gabbling on. Sorry, Isabel. Well, you've heard my exciting news. What's yours?"

I was glad I was sitting down. My head was spinning and I really thought I might be sick.

"Erm… You know the old people's home my mum plays the piano for on Sundays?"

"Er … yes," said Rosie cautiously.

"Mum says that one of the old ladies used to work with the Royal Ballet … and she's, er, going to introduce me."

I looked up. Rosie and Missako were looking at each other with puzzled expressions.

"Well, that's … um … nice, Isabel. Isn't it?" Rosie murmured.

"Isn't it?" I replied.

I stormed into the kitchen and hurled my ballet shoes on to the floor. My brother, Ollie, ducked dramatically.

"Whoah, Mouse! What have those poor shoes ever done to you?"

"Don't call me Mouse," I shouted, fumbling under the chair to retrieve them.

I'd had the worst dance class ever. I had never danced so badly in my life. My feet just wouldn't work. And, of course, Madame had chosen *today* of all days to drop in to watch. Every year she takes a handful of girls whom she sees as being especially talented to train separately in addition to the main classes, and auditions for this elite class were coming up later in the term. For us dance majors it's the biggest honour in the school. The whole lesson had been excruciating. She'd observed my efforts with sharp, dark eyes, her elegant foot tapping until finally she flung her pashmina over her shoulder and swept out, muttering that I'd have to do a lot better than *that* if I wanted to have a hope of joining her elite group. I saw Laura, leaning back against the barre, tracing a circle with a delicate point, smirking.

To complete my rubbish day, Zack was in the kitchen, too, hanging out with Ollie. On the table in front of them sat two giant sandwiches, which appeared to contain the entire contents of our fridge.

"Worrying about your date for the Valentine's Prom already?" Zack took a big bite, as if he hadn't eaten in weeks, and began munching.

"Or did your little ankles go all wibbly-wobbly in your pointy-toe class?" Ollie grinned.

I glared at both of them.

"You are both so … so … *pathetic!*" I snorted, and stomped upstairs to my room.

"Hey!" I heard Ollie shout up after me. "Come on, sis, we were only kidding."

I hated my brother. And I hated Zack, too. I always felt silly and awkward when he was around. Why did he have to go to my school? *My* school! Why couldn't he be at school with Ollie? We'd all gone to the same local primary school, where my two younger sisters were now.

But Ollie was into science and the nearest he got to performing arts was singing in the shower, so he'd gone on to the local comprehensive. Unfortunately Zack didn't. He wanted to act and do music and had got into Linden Lodge. He and Ollie had lost touch in that first year but in the last few months the two of them had begun playing in the local football league at weekends, and it had brought them back together. In fact, it seemed like Zack was around our house all the time.

I hadn't always felt that way about him.

As I flung myself on my bed I grimaced with embarrassment as I remembered back to primary school. I'd had quite a crush on him then. Actually a very big crush, and although he was Ollie's mate, in those days, when he came round he'd always find time to make me laugh, telling me funny stories about his day at school or about his gran. His mum had died when he was very young, and, with his dad away on tour all the time, his grandmother had moved in to help look after him and his younger brother. I thought Zack was the coolest boy I had ever met.

So I'd been really excited about seeing him again on my first day at Linden Lodge. I had bragged to Rosie and Missako that I knew this smooth boy whose dad played in a band. I was also secretly hoping that they'd be impressed by the fact that he was fit and tall with bright blue eyes and blond hair that stuck out at crazy angles. I hadn't seen him for almost a year and I'd missed him. I was looking forward to seeing his familiar face and being teased again.

But I was in for a shock. After scouring the school, I finally bumped into him outside the drama studio on my second day. He was walking towards me with another boy and a pretty, dark-haired girl. I grinned away like a complete fool and said a big, enthusiastic "Hello, Zack!" I'll never forget the look of surprise on his face, followed by his strained expression and his stiff, "Oh … hi." He didn't even stop. I heard the girl whisper something and Zack murmur a reply. The girl sniggered. I stood there, hot with embarrassment, but Rosie and Missako were brilliant and acted as if nothing had happened.

I soon learned that Zack was what the girls in the school called an "A-grader", certainly not someone who would waste time on silly girls in the year below. I had never spoken to him in school again and found it really awkward when he was around our house. I knew he was going out with a girl in his year because I heard him talking to Ollie about her sometimes. Well, poor girl, is all I can say.

I stared at the ceiling, wondering what to do.

It wasn't fair! Rosie always had loads of boys after her. She's tall and willowy, with amazing Irish green eyes and dark red hair – she could go out with anyone. I, on the other hand, fitted the name Mouse pretty well. I'm small, with almond-shaped brown eyes, a turned-up nose and long blonde hair, which I usually wear tied back or piled up messily on my head. There was no contest. Why oh why did Rosie have to like Charlie?

And he may have smiled in my direction a couple of times but what about the next step? Actually talking to him. What if I got all tongue-tied like I usually do? I'm too shy to know what to do around boys. I got asked out a lot when I first started at Linden Lodge, but I was so horrified at making a fool of myself, I always said no. Even if I could get through the talking part of a date, eventually there would be the kiss, and here my brain became a whirlwind of panic as I imagined all the things that could go wrong with *that*. Now the boys had stopped asking (except Gus, who doesn't count as he asks everyone), but I didn't care because I'd been waiting for Charlie to be free. And now he was. And my gorgeous, confident, best friend was going to steal him from under my nose.

I felt a surge of despair and clenched my fists. Not fair! Not fair!

There was a knock at the door and Mum appeared carrying a mug of hot chocolate.

"Are you all right, Bel? The boys said you seemed a bit upset when you came in."

"I'm fine, Mum."

Mum peered at me anxiously, wearing her No-you're-not-but-I-can-see-you-don't-want-to-talk-about-it expression, and put the outsize pink mug down on my bedside table. I smiled – it was the emergency comfort mug.

"Well, if you want to talk…"

"What's the matter with Bel, Mum?" Two blonde heads peeped round the door. My younger sisters had appeared from their bedroom, or should I say small toy shop, eager to hear my tale of woe.

"Has she got no friends?" Abby, the older blonde head, enquired, frowning.

Now she was eight she had been made a buddy monitor for lonely children at playtime, and took her duties as friend to the friendless very seriously.

"Do you want my medicine?" Zoe peered out from under Abby's sleeve, clutching a bottle. "I made it in the garden. It's got leaves and grass and things."

"Bel isn't ill, girls, I think she just wants some peace and quiet, don't you?"

I gave Mum a grateful look, but Zoe had scurried across to my bed and was leaning over, trying to prise open my lips with her small fingers and shoving a rather earthy teaspoon against my clenched teeth.

I pushed it away. "Yeuch! Get off me, Zoe!"

Mum scooted them out of the room on to the landing, where I could hear them beginning to argue about hair scrunchies.

As she went to close the door she gave me a concerned look. "You know, Bel, it's okay to be a private person, but if you won't say what's bothering you, you can't blame people for not being able to read your mind."

I nodded. She gave me a reassuring smile and disappeared.

That is the trouble with my house – people

wandering around all over the place trying to guess what you're thinking. But when I thought about it, Mum was right. I *hadn't* told anyone about Charlie, not even my two best friends. Rosie had no idea of how I felt, so she couldn't *really* be stealing Charlie from me, could she? I needed to talk to someone, so I picked up my mobile and called Missako.

"You know what Rosie told us today…"

"I know! What about that? What do you think her chances are? Pretty high…"

"Missako, I've got to tell you something, something really important."

"Not more surprises! What is it?"

"*I'm* crazy about Charlie, too."

There was a pause. "You never said."

"Neither did Rosie! I've liked him for ages and ages. And now Rosie likes him, too! But she can have anyone! He's just another boy to her – I'm sure she's not really that interested. And I really, *really* like him."

"Wow, Isabel, this doesn't sound like you, you're usually so much more…"

"Reserved," I offered. "Shy?"

"Well … yes, both of those really. I thought you and

I were the quiet ones! The ones who were never going to get to the bandstand."

The bandstand stood in our local park and was either a temple to romance or a notorious snogging spot, depending on how you saw it and who you were with. Most of the school had had their first kiss there. Missako and I were still waiting.

I thought again about Missako and Fred. Maybe she was keeping her feelings to herself.

"Do you think I should say anything?" I asked.

"I don't know … would you go out with Charlie if he asked you?"

"A million times yes."

"Even though you know Rosie likes him?"

"*I* like him, too. It's just that she got to say it first. If she hadn't interrupted me, I would have said it first. Why should I back out just because of an *interruption*? The question is what should I do now? She's always said she wished I would be more confident. What do you think she would say if I told her?"

There was another pause.

"Well," Missako sighed, "it's a very difficult situation, but look, you've been friends for ages. You've always been totally honest with each other until now, so I think you should talk to her. I'm sure she'll understand, and then you can discuss it calmly and sensibly and work out what you're both going to do."

"I *was* going to say it first…"

Missako sighed. "I don't think it really matters who said it first. The fact is you both like the same boy! But I'm sure it can be sorted out."

"Thank goodness *you* don't want to go out with him, too!"

"That *would* make things a bit crowded!" she laughed.

"She *is* going to understand, isn't she?"

"Absolutely," said Missako. "Your friendship is definitely strong enough to deal with a small problem over a boy neither of you even know."

"You're right. And you've been brilliant, I feel a million times better now. Thank you."

"Good," she sighed, sounding relieved. "I'll see you tomorrow."

I put down the phone, sank back on my pillows and took a deep breath. Everything was going to be all right.

"I've seen the perfect prom dress already," Rosie whispered excitedly. "Mum says she's going to make it for me." She pulled a magazine halfway out of her school bag and showed us a photograph of a model in a pale green satin prom dress, with a tightly fitted waist and full swishing skirt. It was stunning. Rosie was lucky – her mum made wedding dresses and could sew like a dream.

"It's all right for you," I replied wistfully. "My mum couldn't sew a button on, let alone make a dress. If anyone did ask me to the Valentine's Prom, I'd have to go in a bin liner."

A cough from Miss Picasso made Rosie push the picture back in her bag fast. Miss Picasso is not her real name, but with her angular face, big pointed nose and huge dark eyes, our art teacher does look a lot like some of his paintings.

It was nearing the end of the day and somehow I still

hadn't found the right moment to speak to Rosie. At lunch we kept getting interrupted and then afterwards I had had to go to see Madame for a talk about the audition, which frightened the life out of me. It was going to be really tough. But *at last* we were all together in the art room.

We had been set the task of designing the decorations for the Valentine's Prom. Everyone in the school was doing it, and the winning idea was going to be announced at the end of next week. Missako's design had black leather and studs and pink net and ribbons covering the walls in stripes. Rosie had drawn a picture of pink heart-shaped guitars hanging from the ceiling. I had enjoyed working on my idea, but my heart was racing as I was running out of time to say something to Rosie. And I *had* to do it. I wasn't going to be the quiet one any more, the one who never spoke up. I was going to let my true feelings out as soon as the right time came.

I didn't have long to wait.

Rosie checked Miss Picasso was out of earshot and leaned forward. "Okay, you two, I need some help with my plan to get some one-to-one time with Charlie. You know he always hangs around with his friends Den and

Sam? I need you to distract them so I can talk to Charlie."

"Whoah!" Missako looked alarmed. "Distract them how?"

Rosie looked at her. "Don't panic! I'm not asking you to do cartwheels or juggle with knives or anything ... I mean by *talking* to them. They're always hanging around the school gates at the end of the day, so I thought we could stroll over and I can chat up Charlie while you two talk to his mates."

"I don't think so," I said in a small voice.

Rosie frowned. "What?"

"I don't think so." I bit my lip.

She sighed. "Look, Isabel, I know what you're thinking, but it won't be embarrassing, I promise; it's not such a big deal simply talking to some boys for a couple of minutes. Come on. Don't you want to help me go to the Prom with Charlie?"

"Um ... not really."

She looked startled. Missako began concentrating very hard on colouring in an area of pink net.

"What do you mean? *Not really?*"

I could feel my face turn crimson, but it was now or never. "Rosie, I need to talk to you. Remember I wanted to say something to you yesterday … before you *interrupted* me."

She frowned. "About the old people's home…?"

"No." I braced myself; this all felt so totally out of my normal character, but I had to keep going. "No, you see that wasn't it. What I really wanted to tell you…" I took a deep breath "…is that I really like Charlie, too. I've liked him for ages and ages, much longer than you have, and I'd like *you* to help me to get him to ask *me* to the Valentine's Prom." I lowered my voice. "I want him to be my first kiss."

Rosie stared at me but said nothing.

I blurted on. "You could get a hundred boys to take you, Rosie. If you hadn't interrupted me at the bench yesterday, I would have said it first. Anyway…" I tailed off, watching her expression "…I'm sure we can work it out as friends … I … er … thought you'd be really excited for me." I pushed my pencil around the table. "You've always wanted me to be interested in boys and now I am."

Missako looked up from her colouring and nodded.

"Mmm. I see," Rosie began. "So, what are you saying exactly? That you believe one boy is just like another to me? That I don't really mind who I date? Is that honestly what you think? That I'm that shallow? I can't believe it. The day I mention I like someone, the *very* day, you decide you like them, too."

"That's not fair! You've been out with tons of boys and I've never said I liked any of them. You only decided you liked Charlie yesterday because he's single again – you're not really interested in him," I gabbled. "But I really, truly am. I've been mad about him for ages … I just kept it to myself, and now all I'm saying is I would like a chance to go out with him so … er … I … I'd like you to … um … leave him alone."

Rosie looked down at the table and nodded slowly. "So I'm not *really* interested in Charlie. Well, thanks for letting me know, Isabel. Thank you for letting me know what I feel and that *your* emotions are so, *so* much deeper and more *real* than mine. It's good to know what you really think about me."

"I didn't say that, but, well, you do go out with a lot of boys…" I said defensively. Missako immediately became engrossed in her colouring again.

Rosie gasped. "Right, I get it. I'm some cheap, loud-mouthed moron with no real feelings, so whatever I say can be ignored and doesn't matter. It's just Drama Queen Rosie sounding off again, so don't mind *her*."

"No, no, I didn't mean that," I cried. "But it was you who always said I should have more confidence in myself. And now I'm trying to, and I'm thinking about what *I* want." I was bright red now. "If you were at all bothered about my feelings, you would have had the patience to actually listen to what I was going to say yesterday before jumping up on the bench and declaring your love for Charlie. It's always about you," I added wildly.

Missako's head shot up. "Hey, come on, you two, this is going nowhere – stop it now."

I could see Joanna had stopped working at the next table and was listening in.

"So that's what you genuinely think, is it?" Rosie looked stunned, then she snapped, "And what makes you think that Charlie might ask you to the Prom?"

"He smiled at me twice."

"He smiled at *me* twice."

Miss Picasso's earrings jangled warningly as she turned towards our raised voices.

"For goodness' sake," Missako pleaded in a low

whisper. "Come on now, you're not really going to fall out over a boy, are you? It's just silly. Neither of you know what Charlie's going to do, so there's no point rowing over it. Let's just forget about the whole thing – *no* boy is worth this."

Rosie crossed her arms and tossed her hair over her shoulder. "Well, it's obvious that Isabel thinks I'm a pretty rubbish friend. And there was me imagining I was being supportive and always trying to boost her confidence. More fool me."

"Well, you succeeded. I *am* confident. Confident that Charlie was smiling at *me*," I snapped.

"He was smiling at *me*, Isabel, anyone could see that."

"I don't think so."

Rosie stared at me before blurting out, "Well, good luck to you then, you'll need it."

The bell went. Leaving her drawing on the table, Rosie gathered up her sketchbook and pencils, stuffed them in her bag alongside the prom-dress picture and hurried out of the art room.

I bit my lip. I had never rowed with Rosie before. It wasn't supposed to have been like that at all; all those angry things we had said. I felt hot tears coming and

clenched my hands into fists to hold them back. Miss Picasso had appeared to see what all the noise was and asked Missako to help her collect the designs. Missako hesitated then obeyed.

Standing on my own I had a sudden urge to run after Rosie, but while I dithered, Joanna appeared at my side. "Wow, Isabel, what was that about?"

I shrugged my shoulders. "Nothing." I certainly didn't want to discuss it with *her*. She'd never been very friendly towards me before.

"It's good for you to stand up for yourself, you know. I couldn't help overhearing and Rosie wasn't very kind, considering she's supposed to be your best friend. Good for you for not letting her walk all over you."

Miss Picasso tapped me on my shoulder, which saved me from having to think of how to reply. "Where's your drawing, Isabel?"

I retrieved it from my bag and handed it to her. She held it up and cast her eye over it.

"Mmm, good idea. I like it."

I managed a smile. Being a confident person was not turning out to be anything like I'd imagined.

It had been the worst week ever. Thank goodness Saturday had come at last. I was in my room, staring into my big mirror, which was decorated around the edge with postcards and photos. Photos of Rosie, Missako and me.

Rosie and I still weren't speaking, and Missako, stuck in the middle of the two of us, had put her foot down hard.

"You are both my friends, Isabel," she explained on the phone the day after the row. "I like you both equally. I cannot listen to you saying anything negative about Rosie and vice versa, okay? That is my rule. I will *not* take sides on this, so don't try and get me to agree with you. I am going to hang out with you one day and Rosie the next. And if you can't say something nice about each other, don't say anything. I can't cope with it, all right?"

She was right, of course. And I wasn't going to do anything to risk losing her as well. But on the days she was with Rosie I felt so lonely. I missed both of them, especially at break time and lunchtime. When Joanna first came and sat next to me at lunch I'd been wary, but she seemed genuinely sympathetic, and in the end it was so good to talk to *someone*. By the end of the week she always seemed to be there whenever Missako wasn't around. But it wasn't the same. She didn't make me laugh like Rosie. I had to remind myself that this was the new Isabel, the assertive Isabel, but when I saw Rosie sitting across the lunch hall making some of the other girls laugh as if she hadn't a care in the world, it hurt.

I wondered if she had noticed that Charlie had smiled at me again, at lunch the day before. Missako had been sitting with me and noticed it too, which proved that he hadn't been smiling at Rosie that day in assembly, or when he passed the bench. He had wished us luck in the auditions next week and said, "See you around."

"See you around?" I gasped. "What does that mean?" Missako didn't know, but then I told her I already had a plan to make sure I would definitely "see him around".

It involved football. Charlie played every week. And so did Zack and Ollie.

And today was Saturday at last. I was going to go downstairs, swallow my pride and ask the boys, incredibly casually, if I could come along later and watch. Charlie would be bound to notice me cheering from the sidelines and then who knows … Valentine heaven…

My daydream was interrupted by the doorbell. That would be Zack. I pulled on a sweatshirt and some leggings and dragged my hair loosely up on top of my head. I could hear Mum singing in the shower as I went along the landing. Downstairs Dad was reading the paper in the sitting room. The boys were already in the kitchen. Ollie was gathering up his football gear and stuffing it into his sports bag while Zack helped himself to some toast. Abby and Zoe were watching them over their cereal. Abby was taking advantage of Mum's brief absence to add four extra spoonfuls of sugar to her bowl.

"Don't think I can't see you, Abby," I scolded.

She stuck her tongue out, unrepentant.

"Have you done your Valentine's cards yet, Bel?"

she asked cheerfully. "I've made three so far but I've got loads more to go."

"Abby! It's weeks away yet! You'll have gone off the boys by then."

"Are you doing one for every boy in your class?" Zack asked. "Because that's very kind of you—"

"No, silly! Not George, he says girls are stupid and he goes 'yakkity yak, yakkity yak'," she wobbled her head from side to side "like that in your face and says, 'That's *you* that is', so he's not getting one. And Duane wipes his nose and puts it on your cardigan when he thinks you're not looking so *he's*—"

"Thank you, Abby, that's quite enough information," I said firmly.

"Are Rosie and Missako coming round later?" Zoe asked through a mouthful of cereal. "I want Rosie to do some 'pressions."

Rosie did impressions of characters from Zoe's favourite TV series and she loved them.

"No. Rosie's not coming today."

Abby and Zoe's faces fell. "Why not?"

I bit into the piece of toast I'd just buttered. "She just isn't."

"*Why* 'just isn't' she?" Zoe wailed. "Rosie always comes on Saturday. You do your beauty faces with Missako and then you go into town…"

"Well, Rosie's busy today," I snapped.

I saw Abby pull a face at Zoe.

I turned to Zack and Ollie. "So what are you two up to then? Playing football?" I sighed in a bored tone.

Zack looked slowly down at his footie kit. "No, we thought we'd try scuba-diving for a change, didn't we, Ollie?"

It was my turn to pull a face.

"We might as well have been last week. Let's hope Charlie plays better today," Ollie grumbled.

"Charlie?" I said too eagerly. "Hasn't he been playing well lately?"

They both looked at me, puzzled.

"What's with the sudden interest in our footie team?" Zack looked suspicious.

"Isabel can be interested in football if she likes," Abby chipped in. "Don't be sexy, Zack."

"*Sexist!*" I corrected swiftly.

"You can call me sexy, Abby," said Zack, laughing. "I don't mind."

I tried to give him a crushing look, which he ignored.

"Why shouldn't I be interested?" I went on. "Abby's right. I might even come down and watch..." I breezed, gazing casually out of the window at the steady drizzle.

"You've *got* to be kidding," growled Ollie. "My kid sister on the sideline? Forget it."

"We are pretty desperate for supporters though, aren't we?" Zack looked at Ollie enquiringly.

"What? *Shut up!*" Ollie guffawed. "You're not to come near that pitch, Mouse. Not even within a hundred metres. Come on, mate." He headed for the door, stopped, turned and frowned at me. "You *weren't* serious, were you?"

I laughed merrily. "Are you kidding!" I joked, suddenly spotting something fascinating on the back of the cereal packet.

"Phew!" Ollie laughed. "For a moment there I thought you'd gone all weird." As the boys trooped out of the kitchen, Ollie returned to his previous conversation with Zack. "Charlie *is* acting odd at the moment isn't he? Must be to do with the split with Laura; did you hear about that?"

"Yeah," Zack replied. "Den told me what he said."

And then they had gone.

What? What had he said? Why had they broken up? If I could find out about that, I might be able to use it to help my cause. Which to be honest wasn't going that brilliantly at the moment. I needed a new plan.

"And that is my new plan," I said to Missako, a few hours later. She was sitting on the edge of my bed. Her hair had been tied up into seven pigtails by Abby and Zoe and they were all sticking out at jaunty angles.

"That is not a plan. That is a disaster waiting to happen," she said firmly.

"It's a great plan and it can't go wrong, honestly..."

"There is no way, *no way*, that I am going to hide with you in your brother's wardrobe so I can eavesdrop on him and Zack. No way! It's the nuttiest idea ever to come out of the nutty idea factory. What's come over you, Isabel? It's like you've been abducted by aliens and have been returned to earth with a totally different personality ... the old Isabel would never do this."

"That's *exactly* the point. This is the new dynamic, assertive Isabel. Pleeeease."

"Absolutely no. This is the old scaredy-cat Missako. I'll just wait right here in your room and you can tell me all about it when it's over."

I sighed, defeated. "Okay then, but will you come with me now to check if I can fit into the cupboard? You might have to shut me in."

"O-kay," she said reluctantly. "But let's be quick. I don't feel happy about sneaking around your brother's room."

Neither did I. I am strictly forbidden from entering Ollie's room and vice versa. I didn't like to think of the trouble I would be in if he had caught us treading carefully through the mess on the floor on the way to the wardrobe. I opened the door. A cascade of faded hoodies, socks, T-shirts, books, old bits of computer, CDs, headphones and half a pack of cards tumbled on to my head.

"Well, that's the end of that idea – you'll never fit in there," said Missako firmly, poking at a pile of clothes with a broken ruler. "Come on, let's get out of here."

We began to stuff everything back in again, and had just pushed the door shut when Missako froze. "What was that?" she whispered.

Zack's laugh sounded from the top of the stairs.

"Quick! Under the bed!" I hissed. I dragged her to the ground and shoved her under. Ten seconds later we found ourselves in a nest of boxer shorts of dubious cleanliness, a couple of ancient apple cores, sweet wrappers, computer magazines and three mouldy coffee mugs. I pulled the bedcover down behind me to form a curtain between us and the room. We were lying facing each other. Missako glared at me and shook a furious fist.

The door opened.

"How embarrassing was that?" Ollie laughed.

"Poor guy. She's not going to give up easily," Zack replied. I felt a heavy bag hit the mattress above us. Missako winced.

"It definitely put him off his game; he missed that strike and it was an open goal."

"To be fair he wasn't expecting to see his ex-girlfriend glaring at him from behind the goalposts, was he?"

I heard a grunting sound and one of Ollie's trainers was catapulted under the bed, followed by a sock. Missako's nose wrinkled in disgust and she clutched her neck with her free hand as if she was being gassed.

Its partner soon followed.

"Charlie reckons she only came to check up that there wasn't another girl watching him this week," Zack continued. "It seems the great Laura can't believe he's actually finished with her and she's not happy. Apparently, he's already got his eye on someone and Laura's got wind of it. I heard she's in the year below as well."

"You're kidding!" Ollie gasped. "*Isabel's* year?"

"Apparently."

My eyes widened; Missako put her finger to her lips.

"Perhaps it is Isabel!" Ollie snorted and barked with laughter. "As if. But talking of girls who *are* in our year, why don't we ever see Susie cheering you along on the sideline?"

Susie! So that was Zack's girlfriend. The pretty singer with long, dark curls in his year. She had been with Zack that first time I had seen him at Linden Lodge.

"Are you kidding? She hates football. I'm beginning to think she hates pretty much everything except being a star and talking about her Sandy audition."

"You and your poncy acting school," Ollie tutted. "You're all so busy worrying about your girlfriends, you're forgetting about the important things, like football."

I heard something being thrown across the room. "Ouch! Okay, I'll shut up."

"Good. I'm starving – any chance of some of your mum's chocolate cake?"

"You're always starving these days. Come on!"

The door banged and we heard footsteps going downstairs.

Missako breathed a deep breath and began pushing me. I edged out bum first then turned and flopped on to my back, staring at the ceiling.

"Phew!" I gasped. "That was way too close! But did you hear what they said?! Charlie *is* interested in someone in our year. Do you think it could possibly, possibly be me?" I sighed.

I turned to look at Missako, but her eyes were fixed on something above me, her face frozen in horror. Slowly I followed her eyes towards the door. Gazing straight down at me, with an expression I couldn't quite read, was Zack.

"It's not what you think," I cringed, scrambling to my feet.

Zack started back. "I have no idea *what* to think. What are you two doing? Why would you want to—"

"Hide-and-seek," I interrupted. "We were playing hide-and-seek with Abby and Zoe and you came back earlier than we thought and ... er ... we knew Ollie would be mad..."

"So you thought you'd stay under the bed and listen to our conversation instead?"

I felt an inch high. Missako had been right, this had been a terrible plan.

"No! No. We didn't hear a word," I protested, "did we, Missako?" But Missako was still doing her impression of a rabbit caught in headlights.

Zack nodded slowly. "Is that right? *Could it possibly, possibly be me?*" he mimicked.

My cheeks burned. I felt totally humiliated, but

before I could respond, Ollie's face appeared around the door. "What are you up to, mate? Did you get your bag?" He saw me and froze.

"They were under the bed," Zack offered. "Playing hide-and-seek with Abby and Zoe, apparently."

Ollie's face darkened. "Yeah right, well they seem to have forgotten about your game because they're downstairs looking after puppies on their Nintendos." He grimaced as the facts dawned on him. "You were listening to us! I can't believe it! If I did that to you, you'd go *mental.*" He paced the room furiously. "Luckily, we didn't have an interesting conversation if I remember rightly. Did we, Zack?"

Zack stared at me. "I didn't think so," he murmured.

I sighed an inward sigh of relief. I couldn't believe he hadn't blabbed and added to my humiliation – it was exactly the sort of thing I thought Zack would enjoy doing. Maybe he was going to save it for later.

Ollie hadn't finished. "You're behaving very weirdly today," he frowned. "First you're kidding you might want to come and watch me play football…"

I saw a flash of understanding cross Zack's face. "Then you're hiding in my room trying to listen to my conversations. What's the fascination with my life all of a sudden? And whatever it is, STOP IT! It's creepy and weird, you freak. Leave me alone, okay? Now GET OUT and don't think I'm not going to tell Mum because I am."

Missako and I scuttled back to my room.

"Well, that's that," I said. "The football team angle is now definitely out of bounds."

Missako sighed. "Don't you think if Charlie wants to make a move he will? It's not like he's shy or anything."

"But maybe he can see *I'm* shy, and doesn't want to rush things."

"Perhaps," said Missako. "And maybe he wants Laura to calm down a bit before asking anyone else to the Valentine's Prom."

"But that's the problem. I'm scared that if it *is* me, someone more confident may distract him and make him change his mind before he gets round to it. What about Autumn Monroe, for instance?"

"Well, he's not worth it then if he's that easily swayed, is he? And anyway, Autumn's never in school. Now she's in that Drama School musical in London she's only around a few days here and there. Besides, the whole world knows she's going out with her leading

man, Joe Johanssen. So that's never going to happen."

"But we all know who *is* going to try and get him … Rosie. And you *know* what a great flirt she is…"

Missako frowned. "Isabel, you know Rosie is pretty miserable about all of this; I think she'd really like to make up. Wouldn't you? You must miss her. I know *I* miss us all being together. A lot. This whole Charlie thing is a nightmare for me as well, you know."

I looked at my favourite mad photo-booth picture on my mirror.

"I don't think she cares very much about what I'm feeling," I murmured.

Missako looked shocked. "I think she does, Isabel, I think she'd love to be friends again."

"Really? Well she's not acting like it. I can see her laughing and joking all over school, even more than she used to. Joanna says it's obvious she's not finding the situation *that* painful."

"Joanna!" Missako cried. "I *saw* you hanging out with her. What does she know about any of this?"

"Pretty much everything. And I think she understands the situation very well," I sniffed.

Missako frowned. "Listen, Isabel … about Rosie, you

know what a good actress she can be…"

"Isabel?" Mum's head popped round the door. "Can I have a word with you, please? Now!" She did not sound pleased.

Thank you, Ollie, I thought. *Thank you very much.*

I went outside and slammed the door behind me.

"What on earth were you thinking?" she shrieked, and then she launched into a long lecture on respecting people's privacy, finishing with, "And are you coming to help me at the old people's home tomorrow? I've been asking and asking, and you did promise…" which was tantamount to pure blackmail.

"Mu-um!" I wailed. "Do I have to?"

She gave me one of her looks. I glowered back.

"It's not the worst thing in the world to do things for other people, you know, Isabel. And it's not like you're going to be the only young person there. Apparently, Mrs Hampton-Smith rang to arrange for a group from your school to do their community work for their Duke of Edinburgh Award at The Cedars. Zack's doing it."

I groaned. "Well, I don't want to go even *more* now."

Mum looked up, her cheeks reddening. I turned round. Behind me, Zack had just come out of

Ollie's room. It was obvious he'd overheard.

Mum frowned at me and smiled brightly at him. "You're going, aren't you, Zack? And a couple of girls and some other boys called Sam and Charlie or something."

My heart gave a jolt.

"Sam and Charlie, am I right, Zack?" Mum asked.

Zack looked coolly at me. "Yes, that's right. Charlie Rothwell. I think Isabel knows who he is, don't you?" He headed down the stairs.

I edged nearer Mum.

"Oh, all right, I'll come," I hissed under my breath.

Mum beamed and called loudly down to Zack. "Good news! Isabel has just volunteered to come along and help, too."

"Really?" He stopped and looked up at us. "You do surprise me," he said, and continued downstairs without a backward glance.

Argh! Why did Zack always have to make me feel so young and stupid? What had I ever done to him? But he wasn't going to spoil this. This was my chance and I had to take it. Tomorrow I was going to be spending time with Charlie, out of school. And I couldn't wait.

As soon as I woke up I checked the beauty outline I'd stuck to my mirror the night before and got started.

1. Drink glass of hot water and lemon juice to detox. (Excellent start – if disgusting.)

2. Shower and wash hair with Mum's most expensive shampoo – remember to put it back in exactly the same place.

3. Put deep conditioning treatment on hair; wrap head in towel.

4. Smother clay face pack over face.

5. Manicure nails.

6. Rinse off conditioner and face pack.

I had to leave the list at that point to manicure my nails again – how long does nail varnish take to dry, for goodness' sake? – then I popped downstairs to boost my energy levels with two chocolate digestives and a piece of toast. I came back up and spent five minutes leaning against my bedroom door because Zoe had chased me up with a jam jar full of her flower-bed mud pack, complete with pebbles and minibeasts and was determined to show me. Then after the pleading on the other side of the door became unbearable, I had to go out and help her catch two woodlice that had escaped from her jam jar and persuade her to take them back outside. We then had to go down into the garden to release them into the wild.

I looked at the final three tasks:

7. Blow-dry hair.

8. Put on make-up. Do not go overboard and look like a clown.

9. Decide what to wear.

I blow-dried my hair and put on my make-up, but I didn't listen to my own advice as I looked like a clown and had to start again. Finally, after another two attempts, I got to deciding what to wear. An hour later I phoned Missako for advice.

"I'm not sure I can give you any, Isabel." She sounded uneasy. "It feels disloyal to Rosie. I know I'd, um, say the same if she asked me. I've told you both that I am going to keep well out of this and I am. *Especially* after yesterday. Quite frankly, you're scaring me."

My heart sank but I knew she was right. I was scaring myself a bit, but I told myself the new me could manage on my own.

It just wasn't anything like as much fun.

"I understand. But please, Missako, don't tell Rosie about Charlie doing his community stuff at The Cedars, will you?"

There was a short silence. "Won't she find out at school anyway? It's hardly going to be a secret. Everyone in that year who isn't talking about Valentine's Day is talking about where they're doing their community work."

"Well, don't tell her that *I'm* going to be there."

I heard a deep sigh. "She's not going to have to be Sherlock Holmes to know that if Charlie is going to The Cedars for a few hours, you're going to wangle your way in there, too. She knows your mum goes there every weekend."

"Okay then, tell her if you have to," I snapped.

"Aaaargh!" Missako shrieked down the line. "You are both totally doing my head in! And oh, by the way, so kind of you to ask how I am. I'm doing just great, thanks!" She slammed down the phone. I tried to call

her back, but there was no answer. I sat there wondering what to do. I had already lost one friend over Charlie Rothwell. I didn't want to lose another. I tried to comfort myself with the thought that, surely, all of this would be resolved soon. It *had* to be.

Mum yelled up the stairs for me to hurry.

I got dressed in skinny jeans, a new white shirt and the highest heels I possessed. I pulled my hair back in a loose ponytail and tied it with a black ribbon.

Mum looked up when I came downstairs. "My, you look very pretty, Bel! Making an effort for the old folk?"

"No!" I replied furiously. "I've just washed my hair, that's all."

Mum rolled her eyes and said nothing. Dad winked at me. "Glad you're going to go with your mum today. There are some real characters there and I'm sure they'll appreciate a little dance."

"What!" I screamed. "A little dance? Mum, I'm not going to *dance!*"

Mum frowned at Dad.

Dad laughed. "Only kidding."

Twenty minutes later Mum's car pulled into the long drive of The Cedars. It was a beautiful grey stone building set in large gardens. Its owner, Mrs Henderson, was standing outside talking to a slight, elegantly dressed woman in a sweeping navy coat. From behind I guessed she was around Mum's age, but when she turned round I could see that, although her sharp, bright blue eyes were set in fine features, she was an old woman.

"That's Mrs Darelle," Mum murmured. "She's the one I told you about."

I nodded, but to be honest I was only interested in catching sight of Charlie.

I didn't have long to wait. As Mum and I entered the stone-flagged hallway, there he was, standing in front of a large vase of white roses on a round table. Dressed in a crisp pale blue shirt and jeans, he was talking to Sam and Zack. Zack, I couldn't help noticing, was wearing the same T-shirt he'd worn all week.

Charlie looked up first and, I know it wasn't my imagination, looked genuinely pleased to see me. In fact his gorgeous face broke into the most dazzling smile. I felt myself go giddy and took a deep breath – I wasn't going to let stage fright mess up my lines this time. This was the new, confident Isabel.

"Hi!" He was actually walking over! "Didn't know you'd be here. How come? You can't be doing Duke of Edinburgh, can you?"

I shook my head and managed to say, "No, my mum plays the piano here on Sundays. I come and help her out every week."

I glanced around. Thank goodness Mum was busy talking to Zack and didn't hear my blatant lie.

"Great! That's great." He nodded, his brown eyes looking straight into mine.

GREAT? Did he just say "great"? I felt myself going red and tingly and light-headed all at the same time. And then even cool Charlie Rothwell must have thought he was going a bit fast because there was an awkward second or two when he seemed to be thinking about what to say next – but at that point Laura and Susie strolled in.

"My my," Laura sighed when she saw me. "Aren't you just *everywhere* at the moment?"

Before I could reply Mrs Henderson bustled up. "Good, now you're all here, come with me into the conservatory so I can introduce you to some of the residents."

I stepped forward to follow, but Mum pulled me back. "I'd like you to meet Mrs Darelle, Isabel."

The elegant woman from the garden was standing next to her. She had taken off her coat to reveal a cream cashmere polo neck and a slim tweed skirt. Her dark grey hair was swept up into a bun.

I managed a smile. "Hello." The woman turned from watching Laura leave the hall and cast her eyes over me.

"Your mother tells me you're a dancer," she said crisply.

"Um, yes … kind of," I murmured.

"Kind of? Kind of?" Her nostrils flared. "Are you or aren't you?"

I looked at Mum in surprise but managed to hold my head up and say, "I am."

She nodded and put her arm through mine. "Good, well, let's go then."

I gave Mum an anxious glance and mouthed, "Go where?"

"Could you take Mrs Darelle to her room, Isabel?

She thought you might like to see her photograph collection. I've told her about your audition for Madame's group – she's very interested to hear more."

My heart sank. Thank you, Mum – what a disastrous romance-wrecking move that was. How long was *this* going to take? I had to be with the others.

"If you want to go with your friends…?" Mrs Darelle was looking at me with a raised eyebrow.

I blushed.

"No, no, honestly, I'd love to see your photographs," I lied through gritted teeth. "Shall we go?" We set off up the wide staircase.

"Who was that girl?" Mrs Darelle leaned her head slightly over the banisters. "The blonde one."

"That's Laura," I sighed. "She's a dancer, too."

"I could see that perfectly well," Mrs Darelle sniffed. "Great technique; no soul I expect. Whereas you, I sense, too much soul but not enough technique."

"I'm in the highest set in my year," I retaliated hotly.

She opened the door of her room. "I am sure, I am sure, but to be truly exceptional, that is something else. That is what we all strive for, surely? If you don't want to dance brilliantly with all your heart you might as well never dance another step."

"Wow." I managed a small laugh. "That sounds a bit drastic."

"Drastic!" She gestured to me to sit down on one of the large white armchairs by the window. "It is simply the truth. The truth quite often is drastic, you will find. Now…" she began to pull out some large albums covered in pale blue silk "…I will show you my pictures and you will tell me all about this audition. Oh, and about that girl downstairs – why do you bother her?"

I raised my eyebrows. "What! How do you know I, er … 'bother' her?"

"I do have eyes in my head and *ears* to hear. I may be old, but I'm not an imbecile, you know."

I sighed. It would actually be quite a relief to talk about Laura.

"Well," I began, "she doesn't like me for two reasons – firstly, she's also auditioning for a place in Madame's group."

Mrs Darelle nodded. "Yes, your mother told me about that. It's important, am I right?"

"Only the most important day of my life bar the scholarship audition to get into Linden Lodge,"

I murmured. "And Laura doesn't like the fact I've been asked to audition. She has a problem with those of us who don't have to pay fees ... and ... um, are younger."

"And the second thing?"

"She used to go out with the dark-blond haired boy downstairs, Charlie, and it's all over the school he's going to ask someone to the Valentine's Prom soon, so she's not very happy about it."

"She thinks this could be you?"

I blushed. "I don't know. Lots of girls would love him to ask them."

I fingered the edge of my shirt. Suddenly I was thinking of Rosie.

"Why do you look so sad about it? He's free, you're free. Why the long face?"

I looked up. "One of my very best friends likes him, too, and we've had a falling-out over it."

"Over a boy! Not much of a friendship then, was it?"

That stung. "It was! It was a great friendship!" And I found myself telling her all about our row. For a stranger she was very easy to talk to and when I had finished she looked very solemn.

"Listen, Isabel, when I was young I, too, was at a

dance school, actually not far from here, and I had a great friend like you, and we fell out over a boy."

"Did you make up?" I asked anxiously.

Mrs Darelle shook her head. "No," she said quietly. "No, we never did." She sat up straighter in her chair and crossed her slim ankles. "And shall I tell you something else, Isabel? I still miss her."

I suddenly felt very low. I didn't want to think about never speaking to Rosie again – or to be still missing her years from now. To change the subject I opened the first photo album and began to turn the pages, only pretending to look at them at first, but then gradually becoming more and more genuinely fascinated. Mrs Darelle had taught some of the biggest stars at the Royal Ballet!

I began to read the newspaper cuttings stuck between the photographs. "Oh my God!" I gasped. "You've trained nearly all the best dancers in Europe! You're *Davina* Darelle 'The Magician'. That's what they called you. That's why I didn't recognize your name straight away. We've got a black and white photograph of you instructing Belinda Blandford on our wall of fame in the ballet studio." I looked up at her in awe.

Mrs Darelle waved her hand dismissively, but she looked pleased to be recognized. "So, how much do you want to be a dancer?" she asked suddenly. Something in the way she said it made me realize total honesty was required.

"With all my heart – it's all I've ever, ever wanted to do. Ever. This audition … it would mean I would have the best teaching in the school on top of what I already have, but I'm the youngest taking it and the others are all having a lot of extra tuition … by private tutors." Mrs Darelle sniffed dismissively. "I know I need it, too, but it's just not possible at the moment."

Mrs Darelle got to her feet and motioned for me to do the same. "Stand up," she ordered.

"What?"

"And take off your shoes." She went into her bathroom and returned dragging a towel rail. I ran over to help her. "This will have to do for now."

"What do you want me to do?" I asked, confused. "Do you want me to hang some towels?"

"Towels! Don't be ridiculous. Why, I want you to show me if you're worth bothering with, of course. I do hope you're not going to be silly about this. I can't bear silly girls. Very tedious."

Which is how I found myself standing on the pink carpet in my bare feet executing pliés and arabesques as best I could in a pair of stretch skinny jeans, in front of an audience of Mrs Darelle and a white Persian cat, who watched, unimpressed, from the windowsill.

I had to concentrate so hard I even forgot about Charlie downstairs. I soon realized that far from this being me humouring an old lady, this old lady seriously knew what she was doing – much, much more so than Miss White, and I thought she was good. Soon I found myself trying my very, very hardest. After half an hour of instruction under her careful scrutiny, she gestured for me to sit down again.

"Well, goodness knows, there's work to be done," she sighed. "I was right, your technique needs a lot more polish and I am afraid that involves nothing else but practice, practice, practice, with a patient teacher."

So not you then, I thought, smiling to myself.

"So I will do it. It will be a challenge for me of course, but I've never run away from one yet. Come here every day after school. We will use the blue room. I will ask Mrs Henderson."

"Every day?" I gasped.

"Of course every day, for an hour; the audition is so soon. Do you want me to help you or not?"

"Yes please, very much. But it seems a lot to ask and we couldn't pay—"

Mrs Darelle reared back as if I'd been sick on the floor. "Please, do not insult me by ever, ever mentioning anything so vulgar again. I will not tolerate silly and I will not tolerate vulgar. Have you got that? Come tomorrow and bring dance clothes. Now off you go and find your friend, Zack, was it?"

"*No*, Charlie. Oh, and I won't be able to come on Tuesday, there's a school trip to London."

"Mmm ... very well, I'll let you off one day. I'll see you tomorrow, my dear."

"Don't you want to come down and join in the singalong?" I asked.

Mrs Darelle gave me a withering look. "Do I look like a woman who enjoys a *singalong*?" she asked.

"Okay," I grinned. "Thank..." but she was already waving her hand so I left.

As I hurtled down the stairs my heart was pounding – Davina Darelle had agreed to give *me* ballet lessons!

And that wasn't all; it seemed that Charlie *did* like me. I knew all he needed was a chance to talk to me alone and he would ask me to the Prom. What a brilliant, brilliant day. I tried to push what Mrs Darelle had said about never speaking to her friend again out of my mind. Surely that couldn't happen? Rosie and I were bound to make up one day soon. Of course we were.

I arrived in the conservatory to find Zack singing an old music-hall song to an appreciative audience. *Typical of Zack to want to show off and hog the limelight*, I thought. Laura and Susie were both watching him, spellbound, totally ignoring the two rather sparky old ladies at their table, who, I couldn't help noticing, were making rude faces at them behind their backs. An elderly man, dashing in red trousers and a yellow shirt, was sitting next to Charlie. When Charlie spotted me standing nervously at the door, he grinned and waved, gesturing to me to come over and sit with them. Laura's eyes slid between us as I made my way over. And she wasn't the only one watching – Zack had noticed, too. I just had to hope he hadn't said anything. He finished his song and asked for some requests and we all sang together. Ruby and Maude, the two friends sitting by Laura, sang loudest of all. I couldn't help wondering how long they had known each other for.

And if they had ever fallen out.

When it was over and it was time for us to go, Charlie didn't get up immediately so I didn't move either. I was trying not to tremble with excitement but stay looking as casual and calm as I could. He turned towards me and had just opened his mouth to speak when—

"Bel! What are you doing just sitting there?" Mum cried. "Come and help us clear up."

I flushed scarlet, especially as Zack was standing next to her. He gave a wry grin. I jumped up and began hurriedly gathering plates, furiously cursing my luck in having a mother who seemed determined to destroy my love life. Charlie *had* to find a moment to ask me to the Prom. He just had to. We just needed a chance to be alone.

"My, that was quick," Mrs Henderson beamed, as I brought the last cup and saucer into the kitchen. "You don't have to do any more. You've done plenty. Susie and Laura can finish up in here now." They looked at me resentfully as they filled the dishwasher.

As I walked back into the conservatory I could see Charlie and Zack stacking chairs.

"I'm just going for a look round the garden," I said cheerfully, hoping that Charlie would get the hint. I walked slowly out into the hall. To my excitement and relief I heard footsteps following me. My heart was pounding. This was it.

"Erm… Isabel…"

Charlie fell into step next to me.

I tried to smile coolly but encouragingly.

"I wonder if I … er … could um … ask you something."

"Of course," I mumbled shyly, trying not to stare *too* desperately.

"Well, that wasn't so bad, was it?" I jumped at the sound of Zack's voice. He had appeared out of nowhere, slapping Charlie on the back and grinning. He seemed slightly out of breath.

My heart sank. What was he doing here?

"You certainly enjoyed yourself, being centre stage back there," I muttered, wishing him far, far away. Laura and the others would be with us any moment and Charlie's opportunity would be gone.

Zack flushed. "Oh yes, of course, you prefer *hiding*, don't you?"

Charlie frowned. "Erm … isn't Susie looking for you, mate?"

"Nope. Got all the time in the world. What about that game yesterday? What do you think our chances are against St Oswald's next week? Pretty good, hey?"

I glared at Zack furiously, but he ignored me. He knew *exactly* what was going on. He was doing this on purpose, but it wasn't funny. It was mean. To my fury and frustration he then kept Charlie engaged in meaningless chat about football until Laura and Susie appeared.

"Better get moving then," he said, grinning at Charlie, "bus'll be here in a minute. Or are you waiting for something?"

Charlie looked around. Laura was watching him with narrowed eyes. He shrugged. "Nope, nothing, better get going then. So long." He smiled briefly at me before walking out into the drive towards the bus stop. Susie gave me a cold, fleeting smile, put her arm through Zack's and followed.

"Bye then, Isabel," Zack called back to me.

Susie and Laura both turned to stare at him.

I watched them walk down the drive, beside myself with rage. There was no doubt about it. Zack had deliberately sabotaged Charlie's chance to ask me out. But why? For a joke? Or because he simply didn't think I was good enough for his mate? Whatever it was, right now he was the worst boy on earth.

"I saw Charlie today."

I was on my mobile, lying on my bed, doing some ankle exercises in the air.

Missako didn't appear to hear. "Did I tell you I've started karate lessons after school?" she said. "They're brilliant…"

"Missako?"

"And can you believe we're going to see *Grease* on Tuesday *and* it's auditions week!" she shrieked joyfully down the phone. "I can't wait! There's going to be tough competition for the lead parts."

"Didn't you hear what I said? I saw Charlie…"

I heard her make a deflated "Oooof" sound. "I heard," she muttered, "at The Cedars – don't tell me any—"

"He was *that* close to asking me to the Prom, Missako, honestly and truly. If it hadn't been for Zack being such an idiot and deliberately messing things up for me."

"Are you absolutely sure he was going to ask you to the Prom?"

"Positive. What else could he have been going to ask me? Why? Have you heard something?"

"No! No! Nothing."

"He hasn't said anything to Rosie, has he? No, he can't have. He hasn't, has he?"

"You know I wouldn't say even if he had. I told you I'm *not* getting involved in this."

"But I *know* he was going to ask me."

"Well, I wish he'd ask someone and then this stupid thing can all be over!" she snapped.

"Will you tell Rosie he's as good as asked me?"

"NO, I WON'T!"

"Okay! Okay! I won't say another word. But I promise you he *is* going to—"

"Aaargh! I'll see you tomorrow at school."

"Missako?" But I think we had been cut off.

When we arrived for drama the next morning, Mr Anderson had put out chairs in a semicircle around the middle of the studio floor.

"This should help you get used to having an audience right up close," he said. "Especially those of you who are of a more nervous disposition." I could feel his eyes boring into me.

I didn't think that was such a great idea myself, and after I had sung "Summer Loving" with Gus, Sadia, Fred and Chelsea and fluffed up nearly every line, I didn't think Mr Anderson did either. I slipped gratefully into an empty chair next to Joanna. Missako was now up, standing in the middle of the room and getting ready to sing "Beauty School Dropout" with Sadia, Rosie and Lola doing the backing vocals.

"Have you heard?" Joanna whispered, her blue eyes wide with excitement.

"What about?"

"Only that one of the biggest TV and film talent scouts is coming up from London for the show. They're looking for young actors to cast in a big film. My mother says whoever gets the star roles in our show will *surely* get noticed. It makes me twice as nervous about my Sandy audition this week. It's so much more important now."

"Wow! That's great," I mumbled, but I wasn't really listening. I was more interested in catching Missako's eye. I owed her an apology for that phone call. Yet *again* I hadn't asked her anything about herself, but it was her day with Rosie and so finding an opportunity was going to be tricky.

"What do you think of Rosie's performance?" Joanna asked.

"Rosie's performance?" I frowned, confused. "Well, it's great isn't it? She's a natural."

Joanna shrugged. "I just wondered if you thought that your situation might be … affecting her performance in any way."

"I doubt it. You said it yourself, she seems to be quite *deliriously* happy these days."

But actually, now Joanna had mentioned it, Rosie *didn't* appear to be her usual confident self this morning. I knew her well enough to notice she was fiddling with her sleeve as she sang, the way she does when she's agitated about something.

After everyone had had a turn, Mr Anderson called us all into the middle.

"So listen, everyone, this afternoon we have the auditions for Danny. Tomorrow night is our school trip to see *Grease*; tomorrow and Wednesday we'll be auditioning for the other speaking roles; and on Thursday, it's the turn of the dancers and auditions for Sandy. Dancers' auditions will be the last session of the day in the studio. Sandy auditions will be straight afterwards, back in here."

Joanna leaned towards me again. "Are you going to watch the auditions for Danny after school?"

I nodded. Of course I was going to! I just had to make it through the rest of the day first. Every class seemed interminably long – even the modern dance class, which I usually love. But finally, the last lesson of the day arrived. We had set places in English and so Rosie and I had to sit next to each other. Five minutes before the end she propped up her rough book, but not before flicking it open ostentatiously in my face so that I could see she had drawn a huge heart with "Charlie" on it. She sneaked a mirror and some lip gloss out of her bag and ducked down to start putting it on. That girl just would *not* give up.

But I was better prepared. I unzipped my pencil case then pushed it towards the edge of my desk so that she could see I had written "Charlie" loads of times all over it in glitter pen. I pulled out an eye-liner pencil, a mascara wand and a small tube of blusher and propped up my text book. The night before I had taped a mirror on to the inside of it. It was the kind of thing that would have made Rosie laugh normally, but not today; neither of us cracked.

By the time Miss Patel had cottoned on to the fact that something weird was going on, we were both as ready as we could be to see Charlie audition. When the bell went we shot out of our desks as if the starting gun had gone off in the 100-metres Olympic final.

Missako caught me up as I arrived at the theatre; Rosie had beaten me to it and was already inside. Missako grabbed my arm. "Look, Isabel, you know it's Rosie's audition on Thursday … I know things are … um 'difficult'…" She peered anxiously inside the theatre where Rosie was already seated. "But I was wondering if you might, you know, the good luck thing? I know she's worried."

It suddenly dawned on me. *That* was what Rosie would be fretting about. If I wasn't there to do the good luck ritual exactly like we had always done it, I knew she'd think she'd do badly in her audition.

"Mmmm… Look, Missako, firstly I wanted to say sorry about—"

"Isabel!" A voice came from behind me. "All the good seats are going, let's go." Joanna took my arm. Missako's eyes narrowed. She paused for a second, and then shot into the theatre.

"What was that about?" Joanna asked.

"Oh, it's nothing really. Rosie has a good luck rhyme she likes us all to say together before any audition; it's a silly thing, but she's very superstitious."

Joanna smiled. "But that's such a sweet idea! When do you do it … this 'good luck' thing?"

"Normally just before an audition."

"But there's no way you're going to do it this time, are you? I mean you *can't*. Not after everything that's happened between you."

I felt confused. "I hadn't thought about it really. I don't know."

"Out, out, out!" I jumped. Mr Anderson was standing centre stage and clapping his hands. "Way too many people in here. This is an audition, not a show. Everyone who's not auditioning for Danny, out, out, out!"

A loud grumble followed, but Mr Anderson was unmoved. Everyone got up and began to shuffle towards the doors.

"Let's try and get in backstage," Joanna suggested. It was a brilliant idea, but when we arrived, Missako and Rosie were already standing there, and in front of them, blocking the door, was Mrs Hampton-Smith. "Only auditionees allowed!" She crossed her arms, doing a brilliant impersonation of Miss Trunchball and glared. Defeated, we turned to go and found ourselves gazing straight into the smiling brown eyes of Charlie Rothwell.

"Charlie!" Mrs Hampton-Smith frowned. "You're late!"

He stopped and looked at us. "Want to watch?" he whispered.

We all nodded. Even Rosie was speechless for once. He leaned forward and said, "Go up to the lighting box. Den's in there. I'll text him and he'll let you in. Wish me luck!" he cried.

"Good luck," we all chorused, as he hurried through the stage door.

Then we heard him call back, "The song's for you." We all craned our necks, but Mrs Hampton-Smith had stepped back into the doorway and he was gone.

We needed no further instruction. We all turned and ran. Straight past the narrowed eyes of Laura Baines and Susie.

Den wouldn't let us talk in the lighting box, so in a way that made things easier between Rosie and me, but I could feel the tension in the air. Surely she had heard what Charlie had said. "The song's for you." Surely she understood that was meant for me? It had to be after yesterday.

I thought Charlie's turn would never come. Finn, Sam and a whole crowd of others went first. When Fred did his audition I looked at Missako watching him and smiling, but if she had any feelings for him she was keeping them well hidden. Then, to my surprise, I heard Zack's name being called. He never said he was going for the part. I remembered what I'd thought about him yesterday, always wanting the limelight, and realized that actually, I'd never heard him talk about any of the parts he got in school.

He sang "Alone at the Drive-in". I knew Zack was good because he'd got the lead in last term's show, and when I saw him on stage I almost forgot who he was.

He simply became Danny, singing about a girl who he thought he'd lost, and you felt he meant every word of it. When he had finished I was furious with myself for being so ridiculously taken in by his acting. It was a relief when Charlie came on at last. Wearing a leather jacket, he pulled the collar up and turned towards us. I leaned forward expectantly, the music started and he launched straight into "You're the One that I Want".

I mouthed the words as he sang them. Was he singing that to *me*? I daren't look at Rosie. She surely must realize now.

When everyone had finished, Mr Anderson came on stage and told them that he would announce the results for all the auditions at assembly on Friday.

I hoisted up my school bag and turned to Rosie. I felt I could be generous towards her now. "Good luck then, Rosie."

She looked up, startled, but suddenly broke into a huge relieved smile. "Wow, Isabel, thanks so much. So Missako did tell you? No hard feelings, hey?"

"Well, well, look who it is." Laura Baines was leaning in the doorway of the lighting box. Her cat-like green eyes flicked over us. "Don't think about coming in here on Thursday, girls. It's my Sandy audition and just thinking of you babies in here will totally put me off. So beat it, okay?"

"I'll be on stage auditioning alongside you anyway," Rosie said coolly, and marched past her with her head held high.

"Yeah, see you onstage," said Joanna, tossing her hair as she followed Rosie out.

I turned and gave Missako a long look.

"Ooh, look at the time," she gasped. "You don't want to be late for your first session with Mrs Darelle, do you?"

"There's plenty of time, don't worry." I took a deep breath. "So Missako, what was it that you wanted to tell me?"

"I am assuming you simply forgot your skirt, Sadia." Miss White sighed as Sadia staggered on to the coach in a pair of teetering heels. "Because if you are under the impression those leggings come anywhere near to being described as 'smart trousers' you are very much mistaken."

"We were told we didn't have to come in uniform, Miss," Sadia beamed, "so I've come as Olivia Newton-John in the final scene of *Grease*."

"Widescreen version," Finn chuckled, clambering up behind her. Sadia jabbed her elbow into his chest.

"Oouff!" He grimaced, staggering backwards.

Sadia bounced cheerfully along the aisle after Chelsea, and then they both knelt up on their seats to have a good look at what the rest of us were wearing.

I don't know whose idea it had been to dress up as characters from the show, but everyone appeared to have made an effort.

"It's not like anyone in this school needs an excuse," Mr Anderson sighed, but I noticed he was wearing his black leather jacket with the collar up. I was wearing black ballet pumps and an old pair of jeans that I could just squeeze into, which I'd cut off below the knee. Then I had put on a checked shirt tied up in the front and, not for the first time, wished I was bigger in the chest department. Rosie and I had often sighed about our lack of volume in that region. She's much taller than me but, like me, she has a dancer's figure – slim and flat-chested.

Sitting two rows in front of me on the coach, next to Blue, I could see the back of Missako's head. Her hair was tied back in a long plait.

Missako wasn't speaking to me.

Then Rosie climbed in, looking gorgeous in a green twinset that matched her eyes and tight pedal pushers. She looked down the coach, spotted Missako and me, flushed and found a seat on her own.

It seemed like Missako wasn't speaking to her either.

I couldn't see Rosie once she sat down, but I knew she was waiting for one person. Charlie.

Yesterday Missako had refused to tell me what Rosie

had meant, so I'd rushed out after her to find out for myself.

"Missako told me what?" I said, catching up with Rosie by the lockers and pulling at her sleeve. "She hasn't told me anything. When I said 'good luck, Rosie', I meant good luck with your audition. What did you think I meant?"

Rosie glanced at Missako, who was now standing beside us, biting her lip. Rosie sighed. "Well, look, I thought she might have told you…" Rosie's eyes darted to Missako before lowering to the ground. "About Charlie."

"What about him?"

"About Charlie hanging around outside my modern dance class this morning, *miles* from where he should have been and miles from *your* ballet class. And if Mr Anderson hadn't appeared and started to go on about my audition, and *if* I had got the chance to talk to Charlie properly, he *definitely* would have asked me out. I know it. I know the signs. He was kind of nervous in that way boys are when they're about to do something like that. I'm sorry, Isabel." She sighed dramatically. "But it's the truth."

I turned round. "Did *you* see this, Missako?" I demanded.

She shook her head. "I stayed behind to talk to Mrs De Silva because, I'm, er, going for the part of Frenchie."

Rosie and I both looked surprised. She hadn't mentioned *that* before. But then again, maybe Rosie and I hadn't been asking her too many questions lately.

Rosie's eyes flashed back to me. "What are you asking Missako for? Do you think I'm *lying* or something?"

"Not *lying* exactly. I don't want to hurt your feelings, Rosie, but you've obviously read it wrong. When I was at The Cedars on Sunday, Charlie actually said that he had something he wanted to ask me, but Zack ruined the moment."

"So he didn't *actually* ask you anything?"

"He all but—"

"Because the thing is, Isabel, you're not necessarily the world's most experienced person with boys, are you? Are you sure you didn't misread the situation?"

I recoiled, stung. "No! I didn't!"

But Rosie had touched a nerve.

What *did* I know about boys? Hardly anything.

Perhaps I *had* read the signals wrong. I clenched my fists. I *must* have more confidence in myself. He *had* wanted to say something to me the whole time we were at The Cedars, I know I hadn't imagined it, and he *definitely* said he wanted to ask me something. I would not go back to being a mouse. I would not back down and give up.

"I may not be Miss Experience with boys," I blurted out, "but there's no need to treat me like an idiot. I do understand English. I *know* what he said to me."

"Don't accuse me of being a liar then. She did, didn't she, Missako?"

"Come on, Missako, you know that's not what I said. I said—"

"I SAID, SHE SAID!" Missako's shout made Rosie and me jump. "Do you know something, you two? I don't CARE what *either* of you said. I have HAD ENOUGH." She slammed her locker door shut. "Forget trying to be friends with both of you. I can't do it any more."

"Missako!" Rosie protested, but Missako was far from finished.

"And another thing – while I've been running between the two of you, listening to you go on and on *and on* about Charlie till my ears hurt, neither of you have asked one tiny question about my life or what's going on with me. Call me weird but that's not *my* idea of friendship. So I'm leaving the pair of you to get on with your stupid fight and I'm going to get on with my own life. You know, the one you're not interested in."

And she'd stormed off and not spoken to either of us since.

And that hadn't been the last horrible thing that had happened last night. When I got home after my ballet lesson at The Cedars, I did something so very, very stupid that if my plans for the school trip didn't work out this evening, my life would basically be ruined for ever.

First of all, I walked straight into Zack as he emerged from the fridge, clutching half its contents. There was an awkward moment as we manoeuvered away from one another and I cursed myself as I felt my cheeks redden. He had this knack of making me feel so uncomfortable whenever he was close. I guessed that was how you felt when someone annoyed you as much as he did. I grabbed the orange juice, poured myself a glass and exited as fast as I could. At the bottom of the stairs I realized I'd left my bag on the table and turned back.

I stopped dead outside the kitchen door as I heard Ollie's voice. "Bel's looking a bit miserable, isn't she? No date for the Prom, I guess. Who are you taking now you've ended it with Susie?"

That was news to me. It could only just have happened.

"Don't know yet," Zack replied. "Chuck me a pen, will you? I want to write down the number of this new takeaway."

"Mmm … hang on…" I heard the sound of a bag being tipped out and realized, too late, that it was mine. Panic shot through me as I raced into the kitchen and lunged to snatch my pencil case from Ollie.

Ollie gave a whoop of surprise and pulled his arm out of my reach. "Look at this! What is this written all over your pencil case!"

"Give that back!" I shouted.

"Ollie…" Zack murmured.

"Looks like 'Charlie' scribbled a zillion times," Ollie chortled. "I can't believe it. Bel's got a thing for Charlie!" He lowered his arm. I grabbed the case and stuffed it back in my bag, out of sight. "No wonder you look so down – as if *that's* ever going to happen. *You*, going out with … I mean, I play *football* with the guy."

Zack laughed nervously. I guessed he hadn't mentioned what had happened at The Cedars to Ollie.

Ollie was enjoying himself now. "Hey, Zack, surely there's some nice Year Seven you could persuade to take her. As a favour, of course. What do you say?"

Zack did his best to join in with the joke. "I could try and use my influence I suppose. We can't have you without a date for the Valentine's Prom, Isabel."

I glared at him. I clenched my fists and in my head a voice was going, *Speak up, speak up, speak up!*

So I did. "Well, for your information I *do* have a date," I blurted out. "Charlie's asked me."

They both turned to me in astonishment. I slung my bag over my shoulder and fled.

As soon as I got upstairs, I flung myself down on my bed, wincing in horror at what I had just said. What had I done? Why on earth had I said that?

And I'd barely slept all night. I was mad with worry about what was going to happen, and in the morning I hid in my room until I heard Ollie leave the house.

So when Charlie climbed on to the coach at last, in his

leather jacket and shades, my whole being was willing him to come and sit next to me. I was certain he was going to start walking towards me, but then Sam's hand shot out and he called for Charlie to join him. Charlie hesitated for a moment, then sat down. I was crushed with disappointment. Still, at least he wasn't next to Rosie – and Laura *was* watching him like a hawk. I was grateful for another thing, too. Zack wasn't around. He'd been off sick today and had to miss the trip.

When we arrived in the plush red and gold of the ornate foyer, I worked my way across the thick carpet to get nearer to Charlie. I could see that Rosie was doing the same, and by the time Mr Anderson was waving his programme aloft and ushering us into the auditorium, we were stalking Charlie like a couple of bloodhounds. I saw Charlie move into a row and broke into a trot. Rosie hurried close behind.

"Oi! Watch where you're going!" Susie snapped, as I pushed past her. But a kind of madness had taken over me. I couldn't bear the total humiliation coming my way if I didn't get to speak to Charlie tonight. Nothing was going to stop me getting to the seat next to his first. Suddenly Rosie's longer legs showed their advantage, but as she shot past me, my arm shot out instinctively to try and pull her back, clasping the front of her top. And then, to my horror, I saw my hand moving away ... and clutched in my fingers, like a long white streamer, was a seemingly endless length of crumpled toilet paper.

Everyone stopped and stared, including Charlie. Rosie's face looked completely horrified. So did mine. "God, Rosie, I'm so sorry," I spluttered. I began to stuff my end of the tissue into my bag. Rosie grabbed the other end and began trying to shove it back into her bra.

"Here let me help you." Laura laughed mockingly. She leaned forward from the row of seats behind us and snapped it in two before dissolving into giggles. Rosie pushed past me and I spun round to follow her, bumping straight into an appalled Missako and Lola, who flattened themselves against the seats to let us pass.

I can't remember much about the show. I couldn't get Charlie's expression of confusion and amusement out of my head. Rosie had stumbled out and found a seat two rows back. Desperately I lunged after her, while a still astonished Lola took the empty seat next to

Charlie. As I staggered to catch up with Rosie, everyone grumbled as I tripped over their feet and trampled on their bags and coats.

"I don't know how she could have done that to you," I heard Laura say as she turned around to face Rosie. "Everyone saw. Did you hear *everyone* laughing?"

The lights went down and the music started. Blue was sitting next to Rosie and I practically fell into her lap in the darkness as I reached them and whispered loudly, "Rosie, I am so, so sorry. You *know* it was an accident. You *must* know that. I would never, ever do something like that on purpose."

She ignored me so I tried again, but again, silence. Then Laura whipped round and hissed loudly, "*Could you please be quiet, Isabel, I'm trying to watch a show here.*"

"Well, you're looking in the wrong direction then!" I shot back, before Miss White hauled me out of the row and made me sit next to her.

I don't know if Rosie managed to concentrate much on what was going on on stage that night. I know I didn't. The likelihood of us being friends again seemed further away than ever. And so did my Valentine's Prom date.

"So, have I got this right?" Abby breathed laboriously as she tried to paint her nails and eat her cereal at the same time. "You pulled loo roll out of Rosie's bra?" She drew back to view her handiwork. It wasn't good.

"But why did she put it there?" Zoe was stuffing her Biff and Chip book in her book bag. "Was she worried they might run out of it in the girls' toilets?" She nodded vigorously at her brilliant guess. "Because, actually, that happened to me at school and I had to shout and shout and Miss Mercer had to come and pass some to me under the door."

"No!" I shrieked. "That is not it at all, though thank you for sharing, Zoe; it's not because—"

"Why then?"

"She wanted to make her bosoms look bigger, silly." Abby rolled her eyes.

"Why?"

"For boys." Abby sighed, quite the woman of the world.

"Abby!" Mum cried.

"But *why*?" Zoe wailed.

Abby looked a bit flummoxed at this, and I decided it was time to change the subject.

"It doesn't matter *why*, the important thing is that she didn't want anyone to know she had… Oh God, I don't know why I tell you anything. I must be desperate."

"Do you have any friends left at all?" Abby asked kindly.

"Obviously not if I'm talking to you two," I replied.

"Bel…" Mum warned.

Abby sniffed, unimpressed. "You're such a crosspatch now Missako and Rosie aren't your friends! I wish you *were* friends again. You were nicer then."

She slipped off her chair and disappeared upstairs, closely followed by Zoe.

"Brush your teeth properly, you two!" Mum called after them.

She turned to me.

"Try and make it up with Rosie and Missako, Bel. I can't believe there's anything so serious you'd break up over it. Seems to me you've all got yourselves into a bit of a muddle this term."

I quoted Rizzo from *Grease*, "'To say the least,'" I sighed, resting my face on my hands. "'The very least.'"

"Can I help?"

"Nooo, I don't think so."

Mum picked up her bag. "Well, I'm here if you need me. Now where's Ollie? He's going to be late."

Ollie wandered in and poured a whole pint of milk into a glass. I braced myself.

"Good show last night?"

I narrowed my eyes.

"The other night, Bel, you know, about the erm … Prom thing. You *were* just kidding, weren't you? I mean I know you were – but if you weren't, you know that would mean he'd be coming round *here*…"

My agonized look was picked up by Mum because she cut in with, "Is Zack's gran okay, Ollie?"

Ollie looked blank. "I dunno. I expect so. Why wouldn't she be?"

"It's just that Zack seems to be around here a lot … and he's eating us out of house and home."

Ollie shrugged. "I haven't seen his gran. Haven't been round there for ages."

"And his dad has been away for such a long time," Mum continued, picking up the empty milk carton and popping it into the bin. She paused, frowning. "Perhaps I should look in."

Ollie buttered a slice of toast. "Nah, he's fine, Mum. Zack says it's great being just them and his gran, she's a real laugh."

Mum relaxed. "Well, that's good. Now come on you two, time to move."

I didn't want to move. I didn't want to go to school. I kept thinking about the loo roll incident. Perhaps Missako was right – I did feel as if I'd had a personality transplant. And I didn't much like my new one. There would be giggling and whispering coming my way today, but it would be nothing compared to the nudges and sniggers that Rosie would have to endure. And it was all my fault. I so badly wanted to go back to the old Isabel; she may have been a mouse but at least she had friends. All this being confident and assertive just wasn't me. I was in this situation because I was so convinced that I was crazy about Charlie. But I wasn't even so sure about *that* any more. The main problem was, I was too scared to back down now.

When I arrived at school, I found Laura and Susie leaning up against my locker. I sighed and slowed down. Just what I needed.

"Hi, Isabel," Laura said coolly.

"Hello."

"A little bird told me that you and your mate, oh no, so sorry, NOT your mate any more, *not* after last night. Anyway, a little bird told me that you two might be under the illusion that a certain boy in our year might be interested in you. Am I right?"

I didn't reply.

"Because I know what it's like for you younger ones and your crushes, but I wouldn't want you to make a fool of yourself. So I wanted to give you a word of warning. I don't know what you're imagining he thinks about you, but you've got it very, very wrong. So leave the big boys to the big girls, okay? You're playing way out of your league."

"So why are you bothering to even have this conversation?" I may have been pretending to be brave but I stood up as tall as I could.

Her eyes narrowed. "Like I said, friendly warning."

"Thanks, I think I've got the message."

She tossed her hair over her shoulder. "Good."

Susie suddenly grabbed Laura. "Look…"

Zack was walking towards us. Great. Another person I didn't want to see.

Laura put her arm firmly through Susie's. "Face facts, he dumped you and I'm not going to let you make a fool of yourself. Don't even look at him, he's not worth it."

But I noticed Laura turn back to give Zack a full-beam flirtatious smile and flick of her famous blonde hair as she pulled Susie away.

"Making new friends?" he asked. He frowned as he watched them go.

"Hardly."

"What did they want with you?"

I shrugged. "Nothing."

He raised his eyebrows. "Really? Nothing. Just a friendly chat, was it?"

"Let's just say that the two of them don't seem to be taking recent, er, relationship developments very well."

"You mean their egos aren't. Pride is the only thing hurt there."

"Do you think?" I couldn't stop myself asking.

He paused and raised an eyebrow. "Let's just say I don't think Susie ever wrote my name on *her* pencil case."

I blushed furiously but I was determined to make him think I didn't care.

"Well, choose better next time," I gabbled, and instantly regretted it. *That* came out all wrong. Rosie would have thought of something a lot smarter to come back with.

To my surprise he simply stared at me and nodded. "I will."

There was an awkward silence. Talking to each other alone was a new departure for both of us.

"What are you doing in school?" I asked, desperately trying to change the subject. "Last night you were so ill you couldn't come to the show."

He shrugged. "I'm okay now."

"You don't look it."

He gave a wry smile. "Don't I? Well, thanks for the concern."

I stared at his crumpled T-shirt and the dark shadows under his eyes and horrified myself with a wild impulse to lift my hand and smooth back his tousled hair. I gripped my school bag tightly. It was the bumping-into-him-by-the-fridge feeling all over again. I had to remember I couldn't stand this boy.

There was another awkward pause. Why didn't he go away? And what was stopping *me* moving?

"Well," he said, suddenly raking his hand through his hair, making it stand up even more. "Like I said, watch Laura and Susie, they're not in the best of moods."

"I can look after myself," I said coolly.

"Yeah, sure," he grinned.

"Yes, I am quite sure actually," I snapped. "I'm *not* a kid. And you're no better than those two anyway."

"What?!"

I hoisted my bag on to my shoulder. "You don't think I'm good enough to date Charlie either."

Zack flushed. "I never actually said that."

"Don't lie! Honestly, listen to yourself!" I cried, suddenly coming back to my senses. "I know what you think about me and I don't care. But I would appreciate it if you would let other people in your year, who *aren't* so arrogant and full of themselves, make their own decisions, okay?"

Zack drew back, shocked. "Look, I'm sorry, you know, if you think I kind of interfered."

"Kind of! You totally interfered. You must be very pleased with your success in ruining Valentine's Day for me."

"Ruining it? So he *hasn't* asked you, then?"

My mouth opened and closed like a fish.

"Isabel! Isabel! Brilliant, another one on my list." Blue came galloping up to us brandishing a notepad and pen. Zack and I stared at her in silence as she beamed at us. "Listen, I've had this great idea which is going to be *so* cool. You know it's Valentine's Day the day of the Prom..." She gave a hysterical bark. "Like of *course* you do. Well, I've thought of this great money-spinning idea – my dad would be so proud! I'm going to go round taking photos of all the couples who are going to the Prom together and then I'm going to stick them on heart-shaped cards and they can take them home as a Valentine memento of the night. It's such an amazing idea, isn't it? Anyway, I'm getting organized early and starting a list, so I'm asking everyone if they're fixed up yet." She pulled off the top of her pen and looked at me expectantly.

I stared at her blankly. No words came out. She raised her eyebrows and turned to Zack. "You?" she queried.

He held up his hands in front of him. "Not quite sorted that one out yet, I'm afraid."

"No worries," she smiled cheerfully. "Loads of people haven't got dates yet, even me!"

We tried to look shocked.

She turned back to me. "So, what about you, Isabel? Got a date yet? *Absolutely* doesn't matter if you haven't. Just trying to get ahead, that's all."

I felt myself go scarlet. I could feel Zack's blue eyes watching me intently.

"I ... um ... haven't quite finalized my arrangements."

"You what?" Blue frowned.

I was in an agony of embarrassment. "I ... um ... don't know."

"You don't know!" Blue peered at her notepad anxiously.

"I think what Isabel is saying is that she's kind of keeping it secret for the time being," said Zack. I glanced up at him, shocked. Was he actually helping me out here?

Blue looked at me. "Really? Why would you want to do that?"

"More romantic?" Zack offered.

Blue looked from Zack to me, and back again. Her face suddenly cleared.

"Oh! *Oh*, I see! Oh my goodness! *I* get it. I see how things are. Don't you worry. I won't tell a soul! Wow! Your secret's safe with me." She hopped from foot to foot excitedly, but suddenly she stopped and frowned at me. "But Isabel, what about Charl ... um..." She looked at Zack, who beamed calmly back at her. "Never mind. Whoo!" She fanned herself with her notepad. "I'm feeling all confused here ... better shut up and get on then. *Loads* more people to ask."

"Blue!" I yelled after her, but she was off at full canter down the corridor.

"Oh God." I leaned against the lockers. "That was a *total* disaster."

"Why?"

"*Why*! Why? Don't you know what just happened there. She thinks..." I kicked my foot hard against the locker "...I'm going to the Prom with you!"

"So what?"

"So what? So number one, if she tells anyone it will get straight back to um, people, and they might believe it and get *totally* the wrong impression."

"And would this be the 'people'," his fingers made quotation marks, "who you said had already asked you to the Prom?"

I went scarlet. "Well, it's, er, complicated at the moment."

"Complicated?" He was standing very close now and it wasn't helping me make a great deal of sense.

"Mmm. Bit tricky."

"How come?"

I felt an urgent need to start rummaging pointlessly in my bag. "I, er, haven't quite made up my mind. I'm beginning to think that he might be the kind of boy who messes girls around, can't make up his mind, playing one off against the other type thing. I'm not so sure I want to go out with a boy like that." I looked up and gazed directly into Zack's eyes and said, "Tell me honestly, do you think he's the kind of boy that would do that?"

Zack stared over my shoulder down the corridor as if trying to buy some time before answering.

Finally, he drew his gaze back to my face. "No, I don't think so," he said quietly. "Charlie's a really nice guy."

I smiled feebly. "Well, that's great then."

"Good."

"Okay."

Zack looked at his watch. "Better get going, stuff to do, you know…"

"Oh sure. Me too. God, what about Blue? How could she think…? Even for one nano-second. I mean some people can't see what's right in front of them, can they?"

"Tell me about it." He gave a sharp bark of laughter and strode off down the corridor.

"Step, step, stop, turn, turn!"

I was trying my hardest to concentrate. It was my dance audition for *Grease* and the studio was full of sweating youths in an astonishing array of leggings, leotards, cardigans and old T-shirts.

We had been practising the routine for a while now and it was lucky I knew it backwards because my mind wouldn't stop drifting back to my conversation with Zack the day before. I kept going over and over it in my mind. Zack hadn't given me a hard time about my lie, which was a miracle – and he'd told me Charlie wasn't a two timer, so why was I beginning to think that if Charlie took Rosie to the Valentine's Prom, it wouldn't necessarily be the end of the world?

Yesterday Rosie had breezed into school as if she hadn't a care. I heard her making everyone laugh with jokes at her own expense. But I knew that she minded inside. Because of audition practices and rehearsals

I hadn't seen her at all today. It was *her* audition straight after mine. I wondered how she was feeling.

As I wiped my face on my towel afterwards Miss White drifted past. "Good job, Isabel," she smiled. I smiled back, pulled my tracksuit bottoms over my tights and leotard and headed for the door. Normally I would have wanted to savour the compliment, but I couldn't think about it now, I had to be somewhere else. I was also trying to avoid Joanna, who had been trying to get my attention all afternoon.

"Hey, Isabel, where are you off to?" she called, hurrying after me. "My mother's coming to watch my audition today. Would you like to meet her?"

"I can't. I'm off to find Rosie."

I was off to get my life back on track.

She gasped and grabbed my arm. "Why would you want to do that? I'm sure she's not speaking to you since the … um … frontage incident."

"I don't want our falling-out to affect her audition. There's something we need to do."

Joanna's face clouded.

"You're not going to do the good luck thing for her, are you?" she asked, astonished. "If she gets that part she'll be with Charlie all the time!"

"Joanna," I sighed. "Rosie is the best actor in our year. She has a real chance of getting the part, and it could be really big for her. You know that talent scout is coming to watch the show. Your mother has a million connections to help you in your career. Rosie doesn't."

"But if I don't get the part I won't *have* a career, will I?" she wailed desperately. "I'll be a failure and what do you think *that's* like when your mother's Paige Madison?"

I stared at her, shocked. "Look, I'm sorry, Joanna, but I can't talk now, I've got to get going."

I dashed out, leaving her standing alone in the studio. Five minutes later, as I was making my way down the corridor to the theatre, I heard a voice calling out behind me. "Isabel Norton!"

I turned. It was a Year Seven ballet major. "Madame wants to see you in the dance studio."

"What? Now?" I gasped.

She shrugged. "That's what I was told. And you better hurry, apparently it's urgent."

I looked at my watch: there were still fifteen minutes to go. I could see Madame and still make the auditions.

But what did she want me for?

I ran up to the top studio but it was empty. I paced around, but ten minutes later Madame had not appeared. After another five minutes I gave up. I ran down the corridor, narrowly avoiding Sadia and Chelsea, arm in arm, in sunglasses and "Pink Ladies" jackets.

"Isabel!" Madame's voice boomed out. "You know we don't run. What's the hurry?"

"Madame, I'm afraid I couldn't wait, I have to be somewhere; I'm so sorry but I couldn't wait for you any longer."

Madame's sleek black eyebrows frowned. "Wait for me? What are you saying?"

I frowned, trying hard to keep still. "You wanted to see me."

She smoothed her neat black chignon with her long fingers. "No, I did not."

The truth was beginning to dawn on me.

"Someone said you wanted to see me."

Madame shook her head and pulled a face.

"No. I did not say I wished to see you. But now we are speaking, I will say this to you – you must try hard,

hard, hard for your audition. You are so nearly there but I have to choose the best…" She frowned and pinched her thumb and forefinger together. "You are so, so close but still…"

I nodded. I understood.

"Now you must go, but this time, no running!"

I walked off like one of those weird speed walkers and the moment I turned the corner I broke into a gallop.

As I hurtled towards the theatre doors my heart skipped a beat with happiness because Missako was there, hopping from foot to foot outside. I knew she wouldn't let Rosie down; she wouldn't let the fact she wasn't speaking to either of us stop this ritual.

"We haven't missed it, have we?" I cried as I sped towards her.

Missako flung the door open.

"She's just been called! She hasn't managed a note yet, she's like a rabbit caught in headlights. Come on!"

We burst in through the doors and ran down the aisle towards the stage.

"What the…?" Miss White and Mr Anderson turned in astonishment. "What did I say about no audience for auditions?" Mr Anderson called out furiously. "Leave the theatre immediately!"

Rosie was now waking up from her paralyzed state and was staring down at us with amazement. Suddenly she began running to the edge of the stage.

Missako and I reached up and grabbed a hand each. We leaned forward and murmured:

"Now we three are holding hands,

We represent the lucky band,

The lucky band before the test

Makes sure you'll do your very best."

We let go. Rosie wouldn't look at me. Missako whispered, "It's a rubbish rhyme, Rosie, I've always said so."

"Not to me it's not. It's my best poem ever. Thanks." She leaned down and smiled at her, before walking back towards centre stage. Miss White loomed behind us and marched us out in front of the astonished eyes of everyone else auditioning. I noticed Autumn Monroe staring at us with amazement with her huge blue eyes. She was back in school today and had been allowed in to watch – in fact now that I thought about it, she'd been in school quite a bit lately.

But I didn't care what anyone thought. Even if Rosie couldn't forgive me, I was just glad I'd done it and I swear Miss White was only pretending to look annoyed.

"What have you been up to?" I asked Missako when we got outside. I was desperately trying to keep the conversation going, but she saw right through me.

"I'm still not speaking to you, Isabel," she said crisply. "Not until you two have properly made up. I'm only talking to you now because I want Rosie to get the audition."

"Well, we won't have long to wait to find out," I replied, peering through the theatre door window trying to listen to Rosie singing. "The cast is being announced tomorrow."

"Will you be Sandy?" Zoe asked.

"No."

"Why not?" She placed one of her ominous-looking jars on the table and an excited beetle scuttled out. Mum had left for work early and Zoe was making the most of it. I made a face at her to catch it before Dad looked up from his paper.

"I didn't audition for it, that's why."

We both watched the beetle scurry towards Dad's bowl of muesli.

Ollie arrived, yawning, and poured himself a bowl of cornflakes. My heart sank – I wouldn't be able to escape him this morning.

"Do you have a boyfriend?" Zoe had become distracted from chasing the beetle and was looking at a picture of Joe Johanssen, Autumn's leading man, in Dad's newspaper. Joe and Autumn were so often in the gossip column I didn't bother to read about them any more, but Zoe had a bit of a thing for him.

"Well, do you?"

Dad's eyes appeared over the top of the paper.

"Dad, there's a beetle drowning in your muesli," I said, glancing at Ollie who was now all ears as well.

Dad peered down. He picked up a teaspoon, scooped out the beetle, and returned it to the jar. "You should be more careful, Zoe, he nearly got swept away by the strong currants." Dad broke into bellows of Dad laughter.

But Zoe was not to be put off by feeble jokes. "So *do* you have a boyfriend?"

I sighed deeply and gazed into my bowl. There was no point in pretending about *that* particular lie any more.

"No."

Dad's head dropped back behind the paper.

"I knew it!" Ollie slapped the table so hard the spoons danced. "I knew you were lying! I knew it!"

But I didn't care what Ollie thought any more. Everything in my life was beginning to spin scarily out of control. The only consistent thing in it was my daily lesson with Mrs Darelle. Her iron discipline was almost

a relief because when I was in the blue room with her, it was impossible to concentrate on anything else.

I still didn't want to admit it to myself, but deep down I knew Charlie was just a fantasy boyfriend. I had dreamed about him like girls dreamed about Joe Johanssen, not like a real person who you'd known for years and who'd teased you when you were a kid and who still hung around your house all the time. But now the whole thing was such a mess, I didn't know where to begin to make it right.

When I got to school, I joined the rest of the class as we filed into the hall to hear the audition results. Blue fell into step beside me, leaning towards me conspiratorially. "I'm so sorry, Isabel. I heard about Zack." She looked around to check no one was listening and whispered, "Don't worry – I never told a soul about you."

I stared at her blankly. "I don't know what you're talking about, Blue."

"Okay, okay." She put up her hands. "Goodness. Whatever you say. So are you back on to Charlie now?"

"Blue!" I shrieked. "Can you *not* talk so loud?"

"Sure, sure," she said, putting her fingers to her lips as we were joined by Sadia and Chelsea.

Everyone was buzzing as we trooped into assembly. Mr Anderson and Miss White walked in looking very pleased with themselves. Mrs Hampton-Smith was, as usual, already up on stage, casting her beady eyes over us, searching for any hint of unseemly behaviour.

Mr Anderson did the smaller parts first, starting with the dancers. And I was one of them! I was pleased. At least I'd get to wear a prom dress after all. Sadia and Chelsea were going to be Pink Ladies and the last Pink Lady, Frenchie, was Missako! Even though she wasn't talking to us she did let Rosie and me give her a hug. Then Sam got the part of Kenickie and Lola got Rizzo. Next came the minor roles. Blue got the part of the headmistress and Julie the deputy head. I saw Joanna biting her lip. I knew it had been her who'd sent me on a wild goose chase in an attempt to spoil Rosie's audition. I'd found the Year Seven girl who had given me Madame's bogus message and she had confirmed it. I wondered how Joanna's audition had gone after all the trouble she'd taken to spoil her rival's. I crossed my fingers for Rosie. Would her rhyme have worked?

We reached the final two parts at last. When Charlie's name was read out I had to stop myself jumping up and cheering at the top of my voice. I was genuinely delighted for him. I could see Sam and Den thumping him on the back, but Charlie seemed strangely subdued. Just modest, I thought. I saw Den lean over and say something to Zack but I couldn't see his face. What a shock for him. I bet he thought he'd be in with a good chance. Autumn was sitting right in front of me and I watched her look over and raise her eyebrows at him and saw him shrug his shoulders in return.

"And now for the final role…" I could see Laura and Susie sit up; I think Susie actually gave a little yelp. I spotted Laura smoothing down her hair as if preparing to be in the spotlight.

"There was very fierce competition this year. We had a fantastic range of talent and some great auditions, but in the end the decision was unanimous. The role of Sandy will go to…" I looked over at Rosie who was unconsciously gripping Missako's hand "…Rosie O'Keefe!"

A huge cheer went up from nearly everyone in

our year. Only Joanna didn't attempt to fake a smile. She looked miserable.

"Ridiculous! She's much too young," I heard Laura hiss through her frozen grin.

"She doesn't have the experience!" Susie replied, clapping wildly.

"That talent scout will just laugh at you all, I'm afraid," said Autumn, whilst smiling and nodding. I was glad that Rosie was too overwhelmed by well-wishers to hear them.

"HEM, HEM!" Mrs Hampton-Smith had returned to centre stage. "And finally, one more piece of news. In four weeks' time it will be the Valentine's Prom and I am delighted to announce the winning theme. We had some very 'creative' entries…" she peered out over her spectacles "…but the winning design belongs to Isabel Norton! Would you like to come up here, Isabel, and let everyone know what it's going to be?"

I thought I must have misheard so I didn't move until Missako dug me in the ribs and hissed, "What are you doing sitting there? Get moving!"

Finally we walked out of assembly, and everyone began laughing and shrieking at once.

"Missako, you're going to be Frenchie and get a solo all to yourself!" Rosie yelped.

"I love, love, love the Prom theme, Isabel!" Missako jumped up and down.

Rosie and I found ourselves in front of each other.

"Hey, Rosie," I said, "congratulations on being Sandy. It's great, really great." I looked around to check no one was listening. "I've got something I need to tell you. Something important."

"Really?" She looked anxious. "Are you sure? Because the last time you said that to me it didn't go terribly well, did it?"

I couldn't help smiling. "You're right. But I think it will be okay this time. I'm absolutely sure it will be. I must talk to you about something – you and Missako."

"Look at those two." Sadia came up and nudged me, pointing out of the window down to the back of the science labs below. Zack was leaning against the wall, talking to Autumn. She was picking at his sleeve.

"Zack and Autumn?!" I laughed. "For once you've got your facts wrong. She's going out with Joe, isn't she?"

"Get with the programme, Isabel! Don't you read the papers?" Chelsea sighed. "They split up weeks ago and he's gone back to Los Angeles. She's a free agent and she's been chasing Zack ever since."

So that was what Blue had been talking about.

"Not for long," Sadia giggled. We watched as Autumn slipped her hand around Zack's waist. "Look away! Look away!" she shrieked. "They've spotted us staring!"

But they obviously didn't care, as Zack pulled Autumn towards him and slowly started to kiss her.

A voice cut in behind us. "If you can peel yourselves away for a moment, Charlie wants to talk to you." I turned round from the window as if I'd been hypnotized and gave myself a shake. Sam stood there, clutching his school bag and looking uncomfortable. Sadia and Chelsea's eyes shone. This was turning out to be a bumper morning for them.

"Who?" I asked, my heart pounding.

"You and Rosie."

"What? Both of us?" said Rosie.

I saw Sadia give Chelsea a "Here we go" look.

Sam shrugged. "Yeah."

"Couldn't he come and find us himself?" asked Rosie.

"He's not feeling too good; he's outside the hall." Sam motioned for us to follow him.

For a few brief moments it seemed as if we had all forgotten that Charlie existed. Now he was back in our lives again.

I looked at Rosie. She looked at me. "What did you want to say just now?"

"Doesn't matter. It's not really important," I lied.

"But you said..." She looked puzzled. "Oh, never mind, come on then, let's get this over with." We set off down the corridor. I was surprised. I thought she'd be much more excited.

Charlie was standing outside the hall, leaning against the wall.

We slowed down and fell silent as we approached. I was feeling hot with embarrassment and I could see Rosie playing with her sleeve. I wondered if she was suddenly feeling as ridiculous as I was. But Charlie *was* obviously waiting to say *something* to someone.

"Congratulations, Charlie," Lola cried merrily as she went past, dragging a protesting Sadia and Chelsea along with her.

She turned back and winked at Rosie and me.

Charlie looked terrible, his face was ashen white and he had a dew of sweat on his forehead. He seemed to be hunched over as well.

Missako had wandered up behind us. She stopped and gasped. "You look awful, Charlie." She pushed between us with a look of concern. "Are you okay?"

"Yeah, thanks. Look." He managed to raise his head. "I think I need to say something…"

Rosie and I stood in front of him holding our breath.

"Say what?" Rosie asked quietly.

He hunched up again.

"I need to explain … about wanting to…"

"You're ill, dude," Sam interrupted. "You need to go home."

"He's right," said Missako firmly, reaching forward and feeling his forehead. "You're burning up. How long has he been like this?"

Sam looked worried. "Since last night, but it's suddenly got worse. I think we should get someone."

And with that Charlie slowly collapsed against the wall and slid on to the floor.

"Do you think he died in the ambulance?"

"For goodness' sake, Blue, shut up!" Finn growled. "Of course he didn't. They'd have told us by now anyway."

"How do you know for sure?"

We were in our form room at the end of the day. We had been told to wait for Mrs Hampton-Smith. Blue swung her legs over the side of the desk and said, "He could have done. No one knows what's happened to him since he left here – he looked pretty sick."

Blue was right. Charlie really had looked awful. When he slid to the floor we had all frozen for a split second and then Missako had leaped into action and rushed off and got Miss White. She'd sent us back to classes but we had all heard the ambulance sirens coming up the drive and then tailing off again into the distance.

"No one dies in real life," Joanna said firmly. "Only in the movies. The real question is – will he be able to do the show?"

We all looked at her in astonishment.

"Joanna!" shrieked Rosie, looking up from some serious sleeve-pulling. Like me, she had been very quiet since it had happened. "How can you say that?"

"Well, it's something to think about. If he isn't well enough to do it, someone else will have to take the part. They're not going to cancel it."

"I hope it's Zack Cartwright," Chelsea sighed. "He's fantastic and sooo gorgeous."

"For God's sake!" I snapped. "We don't know that Charlie isn't going to be able to do it. And *please* not Zack. He'd just love that. He's so full of himself."

Missako looked puzzled. "Do you think? I never thought of him like that. And now I come to think about it, he didn't get *any* part, did he? I'm not even sure he's in the show at all. Now that *is* weird."

"Maybe sometimes people aren't as good as they think they are," I replied stiffly.

"Well, he's bound to get it now," said Lola. She picked up her bag and rummaged for a mint. "Fred, don't get me wrong, you're great, but they're bound to give it to an older boy. Zack will definitely get it if Charlie can't do it."

"HEM, HEM!"

Mrs Hampton-Smith had entered.

Everyone scrambled off their desks and found a chair. She glanced swiftly around the room before speaking.

"Thank you for waiting. I know that you are all anxious to hear news of Charlie Rothwell, which reminds me, I would like to commend Missako for her prompt action this morning. We have heard from Charlie's mother that Charlie has had his appendix removed. He is doing very well and should be back at school in two weeks."

She paused for our exclamations of cheer and relief to die down.

"As the show is only six weeks away this will give him just about enough time to rehearse and perform in it. But we have decided that he will share the role as he will not be able to manage the more vigorous dance routines."

Another cheer. "However, in the meantime, someone will take his place in rehearsals."

Great, I thought, *that's going to be Zack. Now I'll have to be on stage listening to him singing with Rosie every day. Terrific.*

"Fred Donnegan!" Mrs Hampton-Smith beamed at him. "We are going to ask you to step up and take the role. You will rehearse the whole role with Rosie when Charlie is away, then share it with him when he gets back. Is that all right?"

I did a double take. I wasn't expecting that.

Fred nodded vigorously. Rosie managed to grin at Fred, who smiled back, looking slightly stunned.

"I would also like Isabel to nominate three people to form a design committee to help her get her ideas underway for the Prom. It's only a month away, and we must keep up the tradition and make sure the decorations are even better than last year. Being on the committee is a great honour."

I hadn't been expecting that either, but of course I was going to have to choose. I looked wildly around the room.

"We-ell…" I began. Blue was practically bursting in her attempt to convey her enthusiasm for the job.

"Blue," I said. She screamed out loud, clapped her hands over her mouth and then whispered, "Thank you, thank you," at me. She's a bit overwhelming, but the thing about Blue is that organizing things is *exactly* what she is good at. She was a good choice. I went on.

"Toby." There were a few raised eyebrows. I knew that was unexpected. But he was hard-working and thorough and I knew he'd work well in a team. He looked shocked and went bright red.

"And lastly?" Mrs Hampton-Smith said over her spectacles.

"Joanna."

There was an audible gasp. Sadia and Chelsea looked at me as if I was mad. But I knew, in spite of everything that had happened, that Joanna was seriously artistic and creative. I knew she'd be devastated that she hadn't got a part in the show and that she would be dreading telling her mum.

As soon as Mrs Hampton-Smith had gone, Sadia and Chelsea rushed over. "What on earth did you do that for?!"

"Everyone deserves a second chance," I replied firmly. I swung my bag on to my shoulder and looked over at Joanna on the other side of the room. She nodded at me but didn't come over.

As I walked out of the school gates I felt someone grab my arm.

"Isabel."

I stopped and turned round.

"Rosie!"

I was astonished and pleased and wary all at the same time.

"I heard what you said," she panted. "About second chances. And putting Joanna on your team. I hope she doesn't let you down. But it got me thinking." She screwed up her face and gave me an awkward smile. "Well, I don't know what I thought, but I do know that it's been a bit crazy, the Charlie thing. Neither of us know what he's playing at and he's not even going to be around for a couple of weeks, so can we … I don't know, call a truce?"

I felt a huge wave of relief. "That sounds brilliant."

"It does, doesn't it? I mean maybe we could try and be friends again … I know I said some pretty mean things."

"Me too." I wanted to tell her the truth, that I didn't mind about Charlie any more, but instead I said, "And congratulations on being Sandy, you'll be great."

Rosie gave me her biggest grin. "And I wanted to say thanks for coming to the audition. It's been awful not having you around, and I knew you didn't mean the loo roll thing. Congratulations on the Prom theme, it's brilliant."

"And there's another reason we have to make up."

"I know."

"Missako." We both said together.

Rosie pulled a face. "I'm not sure if we've been the greatest friends to her during all this, you know."

"We've been totally rubbish," I said. "I don't know anything about her life at the moment."

Rosie's eyes lit up. "Let's call her this evening and arrange to go into town this weekend."

"Great idea. Oh noooo..." I stared over her shoulder.

"What's the matt—"

"Hi, Isabel." Zack and Autumn were walking out of the gates, arms entwined.

Rosie's eyes widened in surprise. She hadn't heard Zack speak to me in school since that very first day we arrived. She looked at me questioningly.

"Bad news about Charlie," Zack murmured. Autumn flashed us one of her mega-watt fake smiles.

"He's going to be fine," I said firmly, wondering if Autumn *ever* took her hands off Zack.

"Of course he is," she cooed, stroking the back of Zack's hair. Her huge grey eyes darted between Rosie and me. "And a little bird tells me some lucky girl in *your* year might have caught Charlie's eye recently."

"Really?" Rosie gazed at her coolly. "My oh my, what an incredible honour for her!"

"I don't think Autumn meant—" Zack began.

"I think we know exactly what she meant," I said boldly.

Rosie looked at me in surprise.

"I think…" Zack went on, but Autumn wasn't interested in what Zack thought.

"Come on." She tugged at his sleeve, then paused to inspect it instead. "God, Zack, you're so grungy. Doesn't anyone do any washing in your house?"

"Is that the bus?" Zack gazed ahead anxiously. "Come on, I've got to get going."

"I hope *he's* not getting sick, too," said Rosie. "He looks exhausted, but I have to say even *that* looks kind of attractive on him."

"I don't know why he should be exhausted," I snapped. "He's hardly very busy at the moment. He hasn't got a part in the show – they didn't even want

him for Charlie's understudy, did they?"

Rosie stood staring at me wide-eyed. "Er … I see … not *everyone* gets a second chance, then?"

I could see Autumn ahead of us, reaching out to find Zack's hand.

"I don't know what you're talking about," I said. "Look, I've got to go. Mum's giving me a lift to Mrs Darelle's. Shall I phone Missako when I get back?"

Rosie tied her scarf round and round her face so only her eyes were peeking out over the top. "Fine by me," she said in a muffled voice.

It was a relief to giggle.

16

"Where *is* she, Rosie?" It was gone six o'clock, and I'd been ringing Missako's mobile ever since I'd finished at Mrs Darelle's. I stared out of the car window at the pouring rain, grateful that Mum had waited for me.

"I don't know," Rosie replied. "I've tried everyone. Her mum said she was with *you* and I didn't like to say she wasn't. I don't want to get her into trouble. I'm really worried. Where can she be? And why isn't she answering her mobile?"

"I'll try again and I'll call if I get hold of her, okay. She might be with Sadia or Chelsea." There was a pause. "Isabel?"

"Yes?"

"It's great talking again, isn't it?"

I smiled down the phone. "Yes. It really is."

"So are you going to tell me about Zack later?"

"What do you mean?" I asked, as Mum pulled into our drive.

"About why you're so annoyed with him? What's he done?"

"I'm *not* annoyed with him! Well, no more than usual. You know how arrogant I think he is. Got to go." I clambered out of the car and made a dash for the front door.

"Okay, have it your own way. Speak to you later."

I dumped my bag in the hall and wandered into the kitchen to make a cup of tea and grab some biscuits. You needed to recharge your energy after Mrs Darelle.

Ollie was sitting at the table eating pitta bread slathered with peanut butter.

"Oh, hello, it's the winner of the Valentine's Prom theme," he mumbled stickily.

"Bel!" shrieked Mum, coming into the kitchen and giving me a hug. "That's brilliant news!"

"Who told you?" I asked sharply, extracting myself from Mum's grasp.

"Zack. He said I wouldn't have recognized my mouse of a sister up on stage telling the whole school about her idea."

"Did he?" I tried not to sound shocked. "Well, I'd love to chat about it but I've got to make a phone call.

Missako hasn't rung, has she? I really need to speak to her."

Zoe, who was under the table with the tomato ketchup bottle, flour and a bowl of water, gave a little cheer.

Suddenly, my mobile started to ring. I stared at the screen, wishing it to be Missako, but it was Rosie again. "I've just spoken to Fred. Missako's on a date."

"A date! With Fred? We-ell, I always thought she might be keen on him—"

"No! It's not Fred," Rosie interrupted.

"Oh. But then she *can't* be on a date, Rosie. *Surely* she would have said."

There was a pause. I knew we were both thinking the same thing. We hadn't been there to listen.

"Who is it with then?"

"That's the *really* bad news."

"Who?"

"Gus."

"Gus! You're kidding!"

"I know," Rosie went on, agonized. "She's *never* been out with anyone. She'll never handle Gus. He's … well … everyone knows what he's like. Aaargh!

Shudderation! Missako's first kiss *cannot* be with him, Isabel, it just can't."

I thought of all the times Missako and I had imagined what that moment would be like, and it was *never, ever* with Gus.

"Yuck! I can't bear to think of that drooling face," Rosie went on, appalled. "Where would Gus take her on a first date?"

There was a short silence.

"The bandstand!" we both shrieked.

"But would he? Would he?" I tried to stay calm. "It's pouring outside. Surely he wouldn't take her in this weather?"

Another pause.

"I'll meet you at the entrance to the park in fifteen minutes," I shrieked. I was already hauling on my coat.

"Be quick! This is an emergency! The drool could be closing in as we speak!" Rosie yelled in my ear.

Mum gave me a questioning look as I raced down the hall. "Don't worry. I'll be back soon," I yelled, as I opened the front door and slammed it behind me.

Outside it was still lashing down with rain. I wrapped my coat tight, pulled up the hood and began to run down the lamplit street towards the park.

Fifteen minutes later, I was still getting my breath back as Rosie appeared from the opposite direction. We both looked down the path between the dark trees beyond the entrance gates. "It's a bit dark." Rosie bit her lip.

"But it's not that late," I said bravely. "It just gets dark early, that's all. Come on."

Staying close, we broke into a trot towards the bandstand, trying to avoid the puddles and peering through the driving rain.

"Someone's coming!" Rosie whispered, grabbing my arm. "What if it's a mugger?"

"He's moving pretty fast; quick, get behind the tree!"

I grabbed her and we watched, hearts beating wildly, as Gus trotted past clutching his stomach.

We stared at each other and hurtled towards the bandstand, the rain whipping our faces, shouting Missako's name.

And I was so nearly there when I tripped over a fallen branch and fell in a graceless dive headlong into a huge muddy puddle. Immediately, I felt every bone in my body jangle and my clothes turn to ice. Even in the dim park lighting I could see the big gash on my knee through my torn jeans. As I stared at it, my first thought was that I had just ruined my chances in Madame's audition.

"What's happened?" said an anxious voice. It was Missako running towards us clutching an umbrella. "Are you all right?"

"Are *you* all right?" Rosie asked whilst reaching out to help me up. "We saw Gus ... what happened? Please, please tell us you didn't kiss him."

"Let's just say my karate training has not been in vain." She smiled weakly. "I couldn't be happier to see the two of you are friends again, but what *are* you doing here?"

"We came to rescue you," I said, staggering upright. "Fred told Rosie you were out with Gus and we guessed where you'd be."

"But the real question is what on earth possessed you to go on a date with him in the first place?" Rosie stared at Missako expectantly.

Her face clouded as she blew a tendril of wet hair out of her eyes. "He asked me."

"You didn't have to say yes! You could go out with

anyone, Missako. You're stunning," Rosie gasped, as I leaned on her to take a step. I winced. It hurt a lot.

"He *asked* me and I was beginning to think that I was never going to kiss anyone and you were both obsessed with Charlie and only thinking about boys, and I thought I'd better get kissed by someone or else I'd be left behind. So when he asked me out I said yes. I would have talked to you about it, but all *you* two could talk about was yourselves. And once I'd said yes I wasn't sure I was allowed to say I'd changed my mind." She pulled a wry face. "But actually it proved quite easy when it came to the crunch. What with the karate training and everything. So here I am."

"Come here, you lunatic." Rosie smiled, and we all linked arms. I began to hobble between them to the park entrance, but my knee was bleeding badly. "What a catalogue of disasters," said Rosie. "Are you sure you're okay, Isabel?"

"I'll manage," I said, but to be honest I was beginning to feel dizzy and very, very cold.

"There's someone coming," Missako muttered peering through the rain. "Oh dear. I don't know if I'm up to two karate attacks in one evening."

"It is a park … people are allowed to be here," Rosie replied. "And if it is a mugger, he's a mugger walking a dog."

The dark figure strolled straight towards us until it stopped in front of our bedraggled group. The dog circled us, wagging its tail.

"Hi, Zack," said Missako. "Are we glad to see you!" She pointed at my bleeding knee. "Isabel's had a bit of an accident."

Zack stared at us. To say that it was not a welcoming look would be an understatement.

I imagined the last thing he wanted to do was to take Ollie's little sister and her mates back to his house.

"Come on, Zack, please..." Rosie cried. "Look! Can't you see Isabel's hurt her leg and she's freezing. She's going to die of hypothermia if she doesn't get warm and her dancing career might be over if we don't act quickly. Do you want that on your conscience?"

"That sounds a bit dramatic," said Zack. "Can't you just go home?"

But Rosie was having none of it. "Home! That's fifteen minutes' jog from here and she needs dry clothes. How far away are you?"

Zack screwed up his face.

"About five minutes."

"Thank you!" Rosie cried emphatically. "Lead the way."

Zack sighed, bit his lip and turned around. "Come on then."

"Posh, isn't it?" Missako whispered, as we headed up the driveway of a large detached house overlooking the park.

Zack let us into a large hallway. The walls were hung with stunning blown-up photographs of his dad and his band, but beneath them, the black and white tiled floor was covered with muddy boots and trainers, socks, jumpers, old coats and two bikes. The dog shook itself over them and padded muddy paw marks across someone's jumper.

"Er … sorry about the mess," he muttered, as Rosie and Missako helped me over the obstacle course and through a doorway into the kitchen.

Rosie removed a small pile of grubby school shirts from a chair and I slumped down gratefully. The whole kitchen was a mess. Nearly every surface of what had once been a shiny, ultra-modern kitchen was covered with dishes, opened cans, half-eaten apples and old takeaway boxes. "My God, Zack…" said Rosie, looking around with wide eyes. I glared at her. I knew she was going to comment on the state of the room. She caught my eye and said, "Got any warm water and tissues?"

"There might be some tissues in the bathroom," he said, and disappeared to look.

"Wow, this is weird," Missako whispered. "If I was a detective I would make a guess from the empty tins of beans, the dishes in the sink and the general state of things that looking after this house is proving way too much for someone. I thought his gran was supposed to be looking after *him*, but it looks to me like it might be the other way round. When does his dad get back?"

She fell silent as Zack came back clutching a box of tissues. His younger brother, Ted, trailed after him. Rosie smiled at him and then said to Zack, "When we've got the worst of the dirt out she's going to need a shower and dry clothes, too. Do you have anything? Anything at all?"

He looked at me. "You'd better come up to my gran's bathroom and have a shower before we try and sort out your knee. You're shivering. I'll get you some clothes and a towel. Ted," he motioned to his brother, "sit down. I'll get you something to eat soon and don't think this means you're let off homework. We'll do it later."

It felt most strange having a shower upstairs in Zack's house, but I felt a million times warmer afterwards. I put on an old pair of his tracksuit bottoms and a huge sweatshirt that Rosie had left just outside. The bathroom was plain white and neat – someone had certainly tried to keep it tidy. There were some photos on the wall. Old photos. I found myself staring at one of them for a very long time.

"Looking at photos of my dancing days!" A voice from the door made me jump. An elderly woman leaning heavily on a stick was watching me. "That one is me and a friend at The Academy. Well, it was a school then. It's been turned into those smart new flats now."

"I'm sorry. I didn't mean to be rude. I had an accident..." I pointed at my knee "...and Zack kindly let me have a shower. I was just looking..."

"You're welcome, my dear. Since I had my fall, I can't get downstairs very easily, so I'm always happy for some company. Zack tells me he's doing a great job down there. Tell me, does it look all right to you?"

"Gran!" Zack's voice behind me made me jump again. "You shouldn't be getting up on your own!"

"Don't be silly. I've got my stick and I've been in bed all day. I'm going mad with boredom here."

Zack helped her to an armchair next to the bed. I winced as he lowered her on to it.

"I thought I'd better have a look and see what's going on," she chuckled. "I wanted to know who was in my shower!" She beamed at me. "So nice to meet one of Zack's friends. I worry he doesn't get out much because he thinks I can't manage on my own." I watched her trembling hand put her stick aside. "Young people shouldn't be inside looking after old crocks like me, they should be out going to dances and parties and having fun! I know that's what I was doing when I was your age. I wish he didn't feel he has to fuss over me. If only I hadn't had a fall. I've always been able to look after the boys..." A look of sadness crossed her face. "He rushes back from school every day ... I really am a useless old thing."

"Don't be silly, Gran. You're not useless at all. You mustn't worry. You'll soon be up and about again and chasing us around the house like you used to."

She managed a weak smile.

"You're a great boy, Zack." She turned to me. "And it's a lovely school you go to, isn't it?"

"Yes, it is." I nodded.

"Such a shame they're not doing a show this term … they usually do one, don't they?"

"But—" I caught Zack's eye and closed my mouth.

"Not this term, Gran." He smiled and gave me a challenging look. "Shall we get downstairs and see to that leg now?"

"Sure," I replied. "Sure."

"What are you doing?" Zack was watching Missako wrap my leg in kitchen roll after abandoning trying to do it with tissues. Luckily, as I wriggled my toes, I already knew that although it was going to be stiff for a few days, there wasn't any permanent injury to my knee.

"Amazingly, we didn't do kitchen roll bandages in first aid," Missako snapped.

"Here, let me. I've found a proper bandage." Zack came and sat on a chair opposite me, lifted up my leg and rested it on his knee. At once, I had that uncomfortable feeling again. I told myself not to be so ridiculous, but all the same, I couldn't help worrying that I hadn't shaved my legs and that a rolled-up tracksuit bottom wasn't the best look. Zack was leaning right over my knee and I could feel his hair falling on my hand as I held up the tracksuit bottom. As he gently wound the bandage round and round, I made myself think very hard about him and Autumn Monroe.

Suddenly, Zack got up briskly and shrugged. "That's done then. I don't think your dancing career will suffer too much."

"Thanks, Zack. Right, time for us to go." Rosie got up. "I texted my mum to say you'd cut your knee and we were stopping off to clean it up. She'll think you've at least had it chopped off by now."

As we made our way down the front path, Rosie was deep in thought. "Do you know something? I think you've got Zack all wrong, Isabel. I don't think he's arrogant at all, I think he's been doing a great job under a lot of pressure. And do you know what else I think?"

"You think he turned down the part of Danny so he

could get back to look after his gran and his brother after school every day and not have to stay on for rehearsals?"

"Yes I do."

"I think something else, too," Missako chirped up, turning to stare directly at me.

"What?" we replied.

She looked at us both, pursed her lips and laughed. "Er … nothing! Hey! I went on a date with Gus. What do I know? I've completely lost the plot!"

I was beginning to feel exactly the same way.

For the next couple of weeks I threw myself into preparing for the show and for the Valentine's Prom. If I wasn't cutting out yards of pink and gold cloth, or painting large wooden structures, I was at rehearsals after school, skipping across the stage in a cotton dress clutching school books to my chest with the rest of the chorus, or letting Gus fling me all over the stage in the prom scene. Then I had to grab my ballet shoes and head for Mrs Darelle's, who had allowed me to cut down the lesson to half an hour.

"You are making a real improvement." She had smiled at me as I gathered up my clothes the last Sunday I was there. Mum was meeting me in the car and I couldn't be bothered to change out of my dance gear.

"Tell me – where has that boy gone, the one you said Laura used to like? I haven't seen him around."

"Charlie? He's had his appendix out. He's not back in

school for at least another week."

"Really? Poor boy. You must all miss him. But Zack is here this afternoon, isn't he?"

I flushed. "Yes, he is." I was finding it hard to avoid Zack lately.

She scanned me with her sharp blue eyes. "So is that nonsense about you thinking you liked that other boy over now?"

"I, um…" She raised a questioning eyebrow at me. "Yes," I finished.

She beamed and clapped her hands. "But that's excellent news. So you've made it up with your friend Rosie?"

"Sort of. Like I said, Charlie's coming back soon."

"But surely you've told her that you're not interested in him any more?"

I swear the Persian cat on the windowsill opened an eye.

I winced. "Not exactly."

"But why ever not?"

"It's just that I made such a fuss about it in the beginning – I mean a real fuss, and I accused her of all sorts of things – I just haven't had the courage to tell her that I've changed my mind. She might get mad with me again and I just couldn't *bear* another row. I daren't risk it."

"Which of *all* the things I don't like in girls does that come under, Isabel?"

"Silly?" I ventured.

"Indeed. Quite the silliest thing I've ever heard. Now be off with you!"

I headed for the door, but stopped before I got there. "Which dance school did you go to, Mrs Darelle?"

"Why, the Royal Ballet of course."

"No, I mean when you were a girl?"

"A girl? Ah, that was The Academy. I think they've converted it into…"

"Into new flats, yes. Okay then, see you tomorrow."

I ran out into the hall, trying to pull an oversized sweatshirt over my head.

As I struggled inside it a voice said, "Do you need some help?"

I stopped struggling, my head still firmly wedged inside and froze. "No, thank you, Zack," I mumbled.

"Are you sure? It *is* mine, after all."

"Is it?" I felt his hands starting to tug it over my head

and suddenly his face appeared in front of me.

"Hello." His blue eyes were smiling straight at me.

"Hello."

"You seem pretty busy these days."

"So do you," I replied briskly, trying to sound casual. "Better get going. My mum's waiting…"

"Hey, Isabel," he touched my arm. "I just wanted to say thanks, you know, to you and your mates, for not saying anything to anybody about…"

"You need to let your dad know, Zack. It's way too much for you to cope with."

"I can manage."

Mum's horn beeped. "Well, it didn't look like it. I've got to go now. Bye," I cried, and fled out of the house.

My mobile rang as we drove home.

"Hi, Isabel, it's me."

"Missako! Hello! Wasn't it great going into town yesterday? Just like old times."

"It was. It was." I sensed a hesitation in her voice.

"What's up?"

"Well, it wasn't exactly like old times, was it? It was great that you and Rosie are talking now and we did have fun, but there is still, you know, an *atmosphere* hanging in the air between you. An unspoken … kind of uneasiness."

"Hmm," I said, non-committally. "Perhaps it'll just take a bit of time for things to get back to normal."

But I knew exactly what she meant. And I knew that it was down to me not having the nerve to tell Rosie that I wasn't interested in Charlie any more. But there was something about Rosie that I couldn't put my finger on either. It was as if we were *both* embarrassed about something.

And it hung between us until the day Charlie came back.

I was in the art room with Blue, Joanna and Toby when Sadia and Chelsea screeched in at a hundred miles an hour.

"Guess what?"

I put down the staple gun I was using to bunch up some net. "What?"

"You know Charlie Rothwell is back today?"

I tried to look calm and picked up the stapler again. I hated to admit it, but I had been dreading his return.

"I think the whole world knows, don't they?"

"Yes, but that's not it. Guess what he asked Fred?"

"Why are you so brilliant as Danny?" Joanna replied.

Sadia frowned. "No, silly, he asked him for a number from Fred's mobile."

"Fred's got everyone's numbers," I said. "So what?"

"Not just any number, duh. The number of the girl he's going to ask to be his Valentine! The girl he wants to take to the Prom."

I swallowed hard. "And who was it?"

"That's just it! Fred wouldn't say, he's sworn to boy-secrecy and will not divulge. And believe me we have tried, haven't we?"

Chelsea nodded vigorously.

"But Fred did say Charlie's definitely going to phone her this evening, about nine. Just thought you ought to know. We're off to find Rosie now…"

At five minutes to nine, Rosie and I were sitting in my room. Our mobiles lay side by side on my dressing table. It had been hard to organize with parents, but a lot of wailing about falling behind on homework with rehearsals etc. had done the trick. I felt sick and it wasn't with excitement. Rosie looked anxious, too, but I put that down to nerves. I crossed my fingers and wished and wished that Charlie would choose her. Then everything really *would* be all right and she would never have known what an idiot I'd been. She would just think I was being amazingly understanding about it.

Missako appeared at the door with mugs of hot chocolate. I was glad she had agreed to come, too. After all we'd put her through I wasn't sure if she would.

We took a mug each, and sat in a row on my bed. We all fell silent, listening to the steady tick tock of my alarm clock.

Tick tock. Tick tock.

"Brrrrrrrrrrrrrr!" A mobile leaped into life.

Missako's face was a picture of astonishment as we all turned to stare at her bag, ringing away in the corner of my room.

"Go away, Zoe!"

A small arm had appeared around a crack in my door and was waving about enticingly. At the end of it a hand was clutching a bottle.

"It's for making you all pretty for the Prom," she pleaded from the other side of the door.

"It's got half a worm in it, Zoe."

The bottle was withdrawn behind the door for further inspection.

Missako and Rosie were over at my house to get ready. We had showered, shaved our legs, put on face packs, washed and conditioned and blow-dried our hair and were now putting the final touches to our nails and make-up. Like most girls I was wearing my prom dress from the show. Pale blue with a huge frothy skirt. I had had to stop spinning around in it because I kept jogging Rosie as she was trying to put on her lipstick.

She was in green; exactly like the picture she had shown me all those weeks ago in the art room. Mr Anderson had agreed she could have that design and with her red hair and green eyes she looked stunning in it. Missako was in silver with her hair up in a smooth beehive and a pair of silver high heels on her feet. She was looking at a hideously rude Valentine's card pinned above my bed.

"Sweet of Gus to remember each and every one of us on Valentine's Day, wasn't it?" I smiled. "But it would have been good to get a card from someone I actually did like."

"Don't you thank your lucky stars every single day that you didn't kiss Gus that night at the bandstand?" asked Rosie.

Missako shuddered. "Don't remind me."

"Did you know then that you liked Charlie?" I said, battling with my eyelash curler.

"I *always* knew I liked Charlie!" She twirled around the room with her silver skirts floating around her.

"Well, I wish you'd said!" Rosie smacked her lips together in the mirror. "Because you might have saved us all a whole lot of trouble."

"How?" Missako laughed. "I saw how you two were, rowing with each other, not speaking, so unhappy. There was no way I was going to add to the drama. I never thought I had a chance anyway."

"And it was you all along. The only reason he ever wanted to speak to Rosie and me was to find out what you thought about him. He was so totally smitten, you even made the great Charlie Rothwell go all shy."

Missako blushed.

"You've both been amazing about it. I would have thought that you'd go nuts that night he rang, but you both managed to seem really pleased for me! And it must have been such a shock."

"Oh, it definitely was a shock," I nodded. "I thought you liked Fred."

"Fred!" Rosie cried. "Well, we're all okay with it now, aren't we? We're friends again. And that's got to be more important than any boy, hasn't it?"

"I couldn't agree more," I replied, grinning at her.

"Yippee!" Rosie fell back on to the bed and kicked her legs in the air. "Friends again."

"Amazing!" I laughed.

"I know and it's Valentine's Day and it's Prom Night.

We made it, it's ... it's *unbelievable*."

"I'll tell you what is unbelievable," said Missako, frowning, "you and Rosie don't have dates for tonight. And you both look so beautiful."

"Well, hanging around waiting for Charlie to make up his mind wasted a lot of time," Rosie tutted.

"That's true," I sighed. "But at least one of us is going to have a special night."

Missako blushed again – she knew what I meant. "It will be you soon, Isabel. I know it."

I felt a sharp pang. "I don't think so. My perfect Valentine doesn't appear to have found me yet."

Even though he was in my house more and more these days and I spent every Sunday afternoon with him, I knew I still didn't stand a chance. He was dating the most glamorous girl at Linden Lodge, and I was Ollie's kid sister. But I still couldn't stop myself wishing and hoping.

"Girls. The limo's here!" Dad called up the stairs.

We floated down. Charlie was standing at the bottom waiting. He took Missako's hand, staring at her adoringly.

"Oooh, that's sooo romantic," Rosie sighed as we

walked towards the limo after them. "Like Cinderella going to the ball."

"Well, you know what that makes us then!" I laughed.

"I know! The ugly stepsisters! At least they're letting us go in the coach with them. I'm going to the Prom with my best friend, how sad is that!"

"I don't mind. Missako deserves to be happy and she really is crazy about him."

"I don't know how she could have kept so quiet about it."

"Are you kidding? She saw what it did to our friendship and she didn't want that to happen to her. *She* put friendship first." I looked at Rosie. "She was right, wasn't she?"

"So right."

I looked at the ground. It was time to be honest. "Actually I feel extra, extra bad about it all now…"

"Why?"

"Because if I'm really, truly honest, I'm finding it a bit hard to see what all the fuss was about. I mean, don't get me wrong, Charlie's gorgeous and such a lovely person, but…"

Rosie nodded. "You don't have to say any more." She smiled at the driver who was holding the door open for her. "I know *exactly* what you mean."

But as I settled into the leather seats I doubted very much that she really did. Something very like being whirled around in a washing machine had happened to me this term. I had started out being totally crazy about a boy, thinking he was the only one for me, and then I'd realized I'd stuck Charlie up on a pedestal, and the feelings I'd had for him weren't real. But I knew *now* what the real thing felt like, and I couldn't get Zack out of my mind. I wondered what Rosie would think if I told her. Probably that I was mad and the most shallow, stupid girl in the world.

I walked into the hall and couldn't help feeling proud of what I saw. Every inch of it was decorated like a huge pink and gold fairground with helter-skelters and carousels, candyfloss stalls and side shows, all decorated with hearts, lovebirds and cupids firing arrows.

"Wow, Isabel! It's amazing!" Chelsea screeched, running up to me in a mass of pink frothy net. "Blue's so excited because everyone's telling her she's done a great job. Oh, and by the way, she's looking for you, Isabel, she's got something she wants to tell you."

I didn't like the sound of that. "Everyone on the team did well," I said.

"Well, Joanna's mum is thrilled with her and it's certainly given Toby some confidence; do you know he actually plucked up the courage to ask Julie to the Prom yesterday?"

"And she said yes! Yes! Yes!" Sadia had joined us.

"No! No! No!" Rosie gasped. "Brilliant. So are Isabel and I the only girls in our year without dates tonight then?"

Sadia and Chelsea looked over at Sam and Den who were weaving their way towards them with drinks, before nodding.

"Looks like it. Sorry, but if you hadn't wasted so much time over Charlie, I'm sure someone would have asked you."

"Thanks," I said in a hollow voice, as they hurried off to meet their dates.

Rosie looked at me. "Do you mind about Charlie?"

I shook my head.

She pulled a face. "Neither do I. Are we both mad or what?"

"I don't know."

"It's just the last weeks have been so … er … busy, I think I might have sort of grown out of him, or um … something."

"Yes. That '*Um … Something*,' Rosie, I think I know what you mean." I looked over her shoulder. "And I think Mr 'Um … Something' is coming over…"

She started back, shocked. "What are you talking about?"

"Hi, Fred." I smiled. "You look very Danny-esque tonight."

Fred grinned. "Thanks." He stared at Rosie. "Um, I wondered if you might, um … maybe dance … later…"

The lights were too low to tell if Rosie was actually blushing.

"That would be great."

"She can dance now!" I cried, pushing her towards him.

I shoved them both off, into the shouting, crazy throng of partying Linden Lodge.

I could see Missako and Charlie already on the dance

floor. The music was thumping out a rock and roll number and he was joyfully spinning her around.

I smiled to myself and thought how much I had wanted that to be me. Now Missako would have her first kiss with Charlie. And I was actually glad. I laughed out loud when I thought about her close shave with Gus. Thank *goodness* it hadn't been him.

Now I was the only one still waiting.

"All alone and still finding something funny, Isabel?" Laura breezed past. As Madame's audition loomed ever nearer she was getting more and more unpleasant.

"Nope."

She followed my eyes. "See you didn't quite succeed with Charlie," she said, tossing her hair. "I did try to tell you. Though what he sees in her, I've no idea."

"Never underestimate the quiet ones, Laura, there's more to us than meets the eye."

I saw Susie across the room watching us. I wondered where Autumn was. I was dreading her triumphant entrance with Zack.

"I can't understand why boys in our year would be bothering with babies like you anyway," she huffed. "I mean what happened this term? I don't get it."

"We grew up," I said crisply. "Or perhaps you didn't notice."

"Yeah well, we'll see." She stalked off, and I watched her shiny gold dress and blonde hair swinging as she crossed the room. What I had said was only partly true. *Some* of us were growing up. I could see Missako and Rosie on the dance floor. Missako was looking up into Charlie's adoring face and Fred was holding Rosie tightly around the waist. Even Joanna was dancing with Finn.

It was me who was going to be the only girl in the class who had never kissed a boy. After all my efforts to change the way I was, I was still the same old Isabel – the shy one who was still without a boyfriend. I sat down in the corner sipping my Coke and tried to make sense of what had happened in the past weeks. I rejected Rosie and Missako's many kind invitations to join them on the dance floor – I didn't want to spoil their Valentine's evening. I just wanted to get through the night.

A figure appeared at my side. I guessed it was Gus again, asking me to dance.

"Go away!" I said, not bothering to look up. "You've

asked every girl here, and I wasn't even one of the first five, so do you mind if I'm *not* that flattered by your invitation to hit the dance floor. You know I'm going to turn you down again."

"Mmm… Turn me down *again*? I didn't know I'd tried before. Because I think that's something I might have remembered."

My head shot up and blood rushed to my cheeks. Zack was standing over me, tall and cool, his blue eyes staring straight into mine.

"Zack!"

Laura ran up. "Zack! Hi! Where have you been? Do you want a drink or something?"

"No thanks. I'm fine."

She looked down at me. "Well, at least come over to where the rest of us are sitting."

"No, Laura. I'm fine here. I want to talk to Isabel, okay?"

"But—"

"Okay?"

She gave me a daggers look and flounced off. Zack raised his eyebrows and sat down on the empty seat next to me.

"Isabel…" he began. "I wanted to say something."

I shrugged. I was trying to stop my heart racing and my eyes from staring wildly around the room looking for Autumn. Usually she was glued to his side…

His eyes followed mine on to the dance floor. I saw him looking at Charlie and Missako.

"Did you know?" I asked. "That it was Missako all along?"

"Are you kidding?" Zack cried. "I thought it was you. It didn't occur to me he could be interested in anyone else."

I felt unsteady. I took a deep breath and tried to get a grip.

"Where's Autumn?" I asked pointedly.

"Ah … Autumn." He shook his head. "She's not coming."

"Not coming!" My heart leaped. "But why not?"

"Things didn't work out with us. She's gone back to London."

I tried not to smile. I bet that had been what Blue wanted to tell me.

"What happened?" I tried to keep my voice calm.

"Well, there's this girl, you see. This girl I have been

trying very, very hard *not* to want to go out with. In fact, I don't believe anyone could have tried harder than me not to want to go out with a girl."

"And why's that?"

"Loads of reasons, but mainly because for quite a long time she very foolishly imagined she liked someone else."

My face suddenly felt hot and I began to babble. "I didn't. Well, I did. If you hadn't interrupted Charlie that first day at The Cedars he would have told me he wanted to ask Missako out and you could have saved us all a lot of confusion."

Zack held up his hands in mock surrender. "I know, I know. I was a jerk. I just saw him talking to you and the next thing I knew I was running up yakking like a maniac. It was purely instinctive. I kept thinking to myself what the hell am I doing! Why am I doing this? I felt such an idiot. But then I decided you weren't ever going to be interested in anyone but him. I tried to make it work with someone else, but Autumn and me, it was useless from the start. I only kissed her that first time because I knew you were watching from the window."

He looked at me seriously. "I'm surrendering, Isabel. I can't fight it any more. I've kind of known it from that first day I saw you at Linden Lodge, but I was too proud to acknowledge it."

"You were a pig that first day."

"I know. But I hadn't seen you for nearly a year and you were standing there all grown up and ... er ... let's face it ... gorgeous. It was such a shock. I just thought to myself, 'This is Ollie's kid sister, get a grip. Don't make a fool of yourself.'"

"So you gave me a hard time instead."

His face fell. "Can you forgive me? I know we haven't exactly been friends in the past and we've been seriously mad with each other this term, but, well, we do keep coming back to this place, don't we?"

"What place?" His shoulder was leaning against mine now.

"Well, for me, it's a 'I can't get you out of my mind, you're driving me crazy, I want you to stay forever when you wander through the kitchen on Saturday mornings with your hair all messed up but I can't say a word because Ollie's there', kind of place."

"Mmm... I see."

He took my hand. "I need to know, and I'm taking a risk here because usually you're wanting to kill me about something, but I have to ask what place are you in?"

I took a deep breath. "I'm in a 'Why are boys so stupid, haven't you noticed that my hair hasn't been messed up at all on Saturdays for weeks and weeks, and either I am trying to break the Guinness Book of Records for the longest time to make a cup of tea for Ruby and Maude or there's another reason why I'm always volunteering to help out at The Cedars,' kind of place."

He laughed. "I think when I look back, I've had a crush on you since primary school. You were always so sharp and funny, dancing around like some crazy fairy."

"Maybe I had one on you, too," I smiled.

He looked straight into my eyes. "Isabel Norton, do you know how long that makes it that I have actually wanted to kiss you for?"

My heart beat wildly. "No."

He put his arms around me and pulled me towards him.

"Way, way too long."

And he kissed me for a long time. And it was the very kiss I had imagined.

We drew back from each other and smiled, but then I saw two figures approaching over his shoulder.

"Ooops," I warned, "Laura's coming over and she's got Susie with her. They've obviously joined forces."

He leaned slowly towards me. "I don't care about them..."

"But they're going to be mad, they kind of think you're their property."

"Well, I'm not and I don't care what they think."

"And what will Ollie say?"

"I don't care about him either."

Hundreds of pink tissue hearts began to float slowly down from the ceiling and swirl around us like a gentle pink snowstorm.

"You don't care about anything, do you?"

"I care about you. Happy Valentine's Day," he whispered, and kissed me again.

"Break a leg, Rosie!" I yelled through the dressing room door.

"Thanks, same to you!" She came to the door. "Are they there yet?"

"Who? The talent scout or my mum?"

"Both!" Rosie gave me a huge hug. "Isn't this the most exciting night ever?"

I grinned back and had to agree. For the first time in my life I was actually excited about going on stage and not a nervous wreck.

"I'm going to peek through the curtain again," I cried and ran back up to the side of the stage. Through a chink in the red velvet I could see the audience streaming into the hall. In the front row were a few seats with Reserved signs on them. Already sitting in two of them were Mum and Mrs Darelle. I opened the curtain a bit wider and waved.

Mrs Darelle pretended to look horrified. Waving at

the audience – silly *and* vulgar. I grinned as I remembered back to a few days earlier, when I had been to visit her at The Cedars.

I had closed the door behind me and walked across the pink carpet to where she was sitting by the window. The Persian cat had eyed me with its usual lack of interest, but Mrs Darelle's eyes were glinting.

"Thank you for the leotard and the points, they were beautiful, just exactly what I wanted…"

"Oh, for goodness' sake girl, do be quiet about the leotard and shoes. She banged her stick on the floor. "How did it go?"

"We-ll," I began, but I couldn't keep it up for a moment longer. "I got in, I got in, I got in!" I gasped, jumping up and down. "Madame said I must have had a good tutor and I said it was you and she couldn't believe it! But you did it! Thank you so, so much. This is going to change my whole future."

She waved her hand dismissively. "It wasn't me, my dear, it was your hard work. Nobody could have deserved it more, coming here day after day, taking instruction from a crotchety old woman."

I knelt down by her side. "You are not a crotchety

old woman, you're an amazing woman and I want to ask you if you would do something for me."

She narrowed her eyes. "What?"

"Come to my school musical?"

"A musical!"

"Please … I would so love you to be there. Mum will take you. I don't care if you think it's vulgar and silly. Do it for me."

She pulled a face.

"Please. I think it would be *very* vulgar to refuse me."

She raised her eyebrows. "Do you indeed?"

"Yes, I do."

"Then I'd better come then."

And there she was, in the front row. There was a flurry of excitement as a tall, elegant woman was led to one of the reserved seats by an excited Mr Anderson.

"That's her! That's her! That's the talent scout!" Sadia and Chelsea were now peering over my shoulder. "How terrifying is that for Rosie?"

"Yikes!" I cried. "Got to dash."

I ran back to the dressing room where Missako was holding the door open. "Well, *you're* cutting it fine," she tut-tutted. "Hurry up."

We scuttled in and huddled in our ring to say Rosie's rhyme. "It really *is* a rubbish rhyme." I grinned at her.

"Move, move, move!" Mr Anderson had appeared backstage. "Curtain's going up in five minutes."

An hour and a half of singing, dancing and wild exuberance later, the curtain came rippling down. And as we were taking our curtain calls I could see Mrs Darelle standing up with the rest of the audience, clapping and cheering as wildly as any of them.

Afterwards, I was in the middle of shrieking and hugging everyone and anyone in the dressing rooms when I saw Zack waiting at the door and ran to hug him, too. He wasn't alone. His father was standing behind him with Mrs Darelle. "*Do* tell me that he's your young man now, Isabel?" she beamed. "He's such a nice boy."

"He is." I caught Zack's eye. "I think you always knew…"

"Obvious to anyone with eyes in their head. Never going to be anyone else. Now this, this is the real thing, isn't it, Zack?"

"Sure is." Zack grinned. Rosie and Missako came running up to be introduced, and then Zack's dad took Mrs Darelle's arm and we followed them back through the warren of dressing rooms backstage and out into the hall where Mum was waiting, looking embarrassingly proud.

"You've grown up so much!" she cried as she gave me a big hug.

"That was excellent entertainment," Mrs Darelle stated as we made our way outside. She climbed into the back of the car with Rosie and Missako. "Rosie, you are a wonderful actress; I was sitting next to a woman who wrote furious notes every time you appeared."

"That was one of the biggest talent scouts in the country," Mum said, as she turned the car towards the park.

"Really? Well, she put 'Juliet' and a question mark in capital letters."

Rosie shrieked. "Oh my God, it's the new Shakespeare film – they've already cast Joe Johanssen for Romeo. It's why he went back to Los Angeles."

"You're going to be famous!" I yelled.

"Here we are." Mum pulled up in front of Zack's

house. Zack's dad's black convertible was already parked in the driveway.

Mrs Darelle looked through the car window and frowned. "But this isn't The Cedars."

"We're just stopping at Zack's house for a moment."

I helped a puzzled Mrs Darelle out of the car.

Zack's dad opened the door on to a spotlessly tidy hall and pushed open the kitchen door. I didn't recognize it. Every surface shone and the ceiling was festooned with balloons and decorations.

"Surprise! Happy Birthday!"

On the table stood a huge birthday tea with a cake with a ballerina on it. Next to it was a pile of presents.

Mrs Darelle looked furious. "How did you know?" she cried. "I can't bear a fuss."

"Well, you're going to get one anyway," I said. "So you might as well enjoy it."

"Why don't you sit down and open your presents," Mum suggested.

She opened chocolates and cashmere socks and a pashmina and then she came to mine and frowned, holding it up. "I don't understand, Isabel, this is my photograph. Is it from my collection?"

"No, Davina," a voice said from the door, "it's from mine."

Zack's gran was standing there, resplendent in a scarlet dress and large pearl necklace.

Mrs Darelle stared for what seemed like an eternity before saying, "Well, well, well, Geraldine, you never could resist a dramatic entrance, could you?"

"Aren't you going to tell me my dress is hideous and much too loud?"

"No, but you are."

They both burst out laughing. "I can't believe we've found each other again after all these years," Zack's gran beamed. "And it's just as well, as you never did know how to have proper fun without me!" She turned to me. "How clever of you to spot the photo on my wall."

I smiled. "It was all down to chance – if I hadn't been such a klutz and fallen over, I'd never have seen it. But tell me, whatever happened to the boy – you know the one you fell out over all those years ago?"

The two old women looked at each other sheepishly.

"He went off with that Hettie Barker, didn't he?" Mrs Darelle sighed.

"Right under our noses!" They began to giggle. I was getting used to the shocking sight of Mrs Darelle giggling. She had hardly stopped all evening.

Later Zack, Rosie, Missako and I congregated around the last of the birthday cake.

"I would like to make a toast!" said Rosie, raising her glass of lemonade. "To the happy return of your dad and the arrival of your new Swedish housekeeper!"

We raised our glasses.

"Was he very mad with you for not telling him what was going on?" Missako asked.

"Yes, but kind of proud of me, too. He was most angry about me not being in the show. But there'll be other shows. Talking of which, I think I can hear Ted playing my new guitar." He disappeared out of the room.

"I've got another toast," I said, waving my glass around. "To us!"

"To us!" Rosie and Missako cheered.

Rosie suddenly looked solemn. "There nearly wasn't an 'us', was there? We nearly messed up big time."

"Please don't ever, ever stop being warm-hearted and outrageous and hilarious, Rosie," I smiled.

"And please don't ever stop being sensitive and wise and kind and funny," she replied

"We'll never let anything stand in the way of our friendship again, will we?" Missako said.

"Never!" I yelled, banging my glass on the table. Everyone turned round to look, but strangely I didn't feel shy about it. Maybe I had grown up after all. I gazed at all the people in the room. "Final toast," I cried. "To friendship."

Rosie and Missako grinned up at me and the whole room yelled, "To friendship."

"And staying together!" Zack's gran cried.

Clearing up later, I was startled to be hustled into the darkness of the hall by my lovely new boyfriend.

"Zack! What are you doing?" I laughed.

"I would like to propose another toast," he said, putting his arms around me.

"To what?" I asked.

"To you and me," he replied. "And staying together." And he kissed me for the longest time.

And look out for the next Crush Confidential title:

Slippery slopes, high hopes
and my winter dream boy